STACY GREGG grew up training her bewildered dog to showjump in the backyard until her parents gave in to her desperate pleas and finally let her have a pony. Stacy's ponies and her experiences at her local pony club were the inspiration for the *Pony Club Secrets* books, and her later years at boarding school became the catalyst for the *Pony Club Rivals* series.

Pictured here with her beloved Dutch Warmblood gelding, Ash, Stacy is a board member of the Horse Welfare Auxiliary.

Find out more at: www.stacygregg.co.uk

The Pony Club Rivals series:

PONY CLUB RIVALS
RIVALS
The Prize

STACY GREGG

HarperCollins *Children's Books*

For Isadora, who was just a baby when I wrote my first book and is now old enough to apply for Blainford Academy. I hope your future is full of ponies and happiness.

www.stacygregg.co.uk

First published in Great Britain by HarperCollins *Children's Books* in 2011
HarperCollins *Children's Books* is a division of HarperCollins*Publishers* Ltd,
77-85 Fulham Palace Road, Hammersmith, London, W6 8JB

1

Text copyright © Stacy Gregg 2011

ISBN 978-0-00-733346-2

Stacy Gregg asserts the moral right to be identified
as the author of the work.

Typeset in 11.5/20pt Palatino by Palimpsest Book Production Limited,
Falkirk, Stirlingshire
Printed and bound in England by Clays Ltd, St Ives plc

Chapter One

*D*ominic Blackwell was a phenomenon. Blessed with aristocratic good looks and a talent for magically coaxing a clear round out of the most temperamental and difficult horses, he was the rock star of the showjumping circuit. His fans utterly adored him. Girls had posters of him on their bedroom walls and in his hometown of Kentucky, he often got a standing ovation when he entered the arena.

"They wouldn't be so mad about the big jerk if they actually knew him," his head girl, Louise, muttered under her breath. She was waiting anxiously in the wings of the Kentucky Horse Park stadium, holding the reins of Dominic Blackwell's big grey stallion, Maximillion, looking out at the crowd of more than ten thousand in the grandstand. Any moment now Dominic was due to ride his crucial final speed round on Maxi. The only problem was, he was nowhere to be seen.

A sudden roar rose up from the crowd in the stadium and the voice of announcer Jilly Jones came over the loudspeaker.

"An unfortunate four faults for Penny Simpson on Delphine! And now our last rider in this final speed round; Dominic Blackwell on Revel's Maximillion."

They were calling him into the ring! Louise's eyes scanned the warm-up area, her heart racing. Where was Dominic? She'd sent Frannie the junior groom off to find him and now Frannie had disappeared too! Now Louise was stuck here, holding on to the enormous grey Holsteiner. Any minute now they would be disqualifying her boss for failing to turn up and…

"Louise!"

It was Dominic at last. He was striding towards her over the soft sawdust of the warm-up arena, a dark scowl on his face, with Frannie scurrying along in his wake looking flushed with anxiety.

"Why aren't you onboard Maxi warming him up?" he snarled.

"What?" Louise was horrified. Dominic had given her specific orders that on no account was she allowed to ride Maxi, however, she knew that contradicting her boss wasn't an option.

"I'm sorry, Dominic," she said and swallowed her pride.

"Use your common sense," Dominic Blackwell snarled at his head groom. "I'm going to have to take him into the ring cold now."

He snatched the reins out of her hand and glared at Frannie who was standing by nervously. "Well, come on, girl! Leg me up!"

Frannie gave a grunt as she lifted the man who was almost twice her size into the saddle and he jabbed her in the face with his knee. Without an apology or backwards glance, Dominic Blackwell wheeled the grey stallion about and headed into the ring.

The two grooms watched as their boss entered the arena to thunderous applause. A moment ago Dominic had a face like thunder, but as soon as he was in front of the crowds he was the smiling, cheerful Dominic Blackwell that fans knew and adored. He gave a friendly wave to the grandstand as he did a lap around the perimeter.

"And here he is," Jilly Jones trilled, "Local Kentucky boy and a former pupil of Blainford Academy, Dominic Blackwell. You may have noticed his red jacket; that denotes his status as a member of the United States international showjumping team. Dominic is only twenty-eight years of age but he has already won gold at the last Olympics and the horse he is riding today looks set to compete at the next games in Rome. Many are calling this horse the best in his stable, the ten-year-old stallion Revel's Maximillion!"

In the wings of the stadium, Louise felt sick as she watched her boss ride towards the first fence. The fences in this Grand Prix arena were the full height of a metre sixty and even a horse with the class and grace of Maxi required a warm-up to get over jumps of that height.

Maxi made a plucky attempt at the first fence but he took down the top rail with his hind legs. The crowd let out an audible cry of dismay. Louise kept her eyes glued on Dominic's expression. His smile had slipped a bit but he still had his game face on. He came into the second fence and rode it perfectly, but yet again Maxi dragged a hind leg and another rail went down. Dominic's smile was replaced by a grimace. He turned the grey towards the next fence – a very wide red and green striped oxer – and rode at it for all he was worth. Maxi cleared this one with a grunt of effort and before they had even landed Dominic was looking to the next fence. In three quick strides they were at the blue and white upright. It was also set at the maximum height of a metre sixty but Maxi flew it with air to spare. The big grey was in the groove now and he took the wide, wide spread of the water jump with ease, popped the double with no trouble, put in a brilliant leap over the Swedish oxer and came in on a perfect stride to the triple. The last two fences gave him no problems either and he was home through the flags on a time of one minute and twenty-three seconds.

"It's a good time," Jilly Jones told the crowds, "but with those early eight faults it doesn't matter. Dominic Blackwell and Revel's Maximillion slip all the way down the leaderboard to ninth place and out of contention for the considerable prize money and the trophy here at Kentucky."

Waiting in the wings, Louise steeled herself for the worst. In the three months that she had been working as head girl for Dominic Blackwell she had never seen her boss lose. The expression on his face was fearful as he rode out of the arena, his eyes black with fury.

Frannie reached out a hand to take Maxi's reins, expecting Dominic to slow down, but he trotted straight at her and she had to leap aside to let Maxi past! Both girls cast a glance at each other and then began to run after the big Holsteiner.

When they had reached the sanctuary of the stable block, Dominic performed a flying dismount and threw the reins at a puffed, exhausted Frannie.

He was still bristling with uncontrollable, violent anger, but he managed to resist taking it out on his horse. Instead, he stormed off in a huff and, out of sight of the other riders or crowds, he began to thrash at the ground with his riding crop. In a blind rage he rained down blow after blow until the whip broke in his hand, then Dominic dropped to his knees, a spent force exhausted by his own fury.

His two grooms knew better than to try and comfort him. "Let's get out of here…" Louise told Frannie.

Taking Maxi's reins, she turned the grey stallion to head for the stables when Dominic rose up off his knees and turned to her.

"Head girl!" he barked, "Come here!"

Louise handed Frannie back the reins and took a reluctant step towards her employer. "Yes, Dominic?"

"Why didn't you warm the horse up like I told you to?" Dominic asked through gritted teeth.

Louise didn't know what to say. Dominic had specifically ordered her *not* to warm up Maxi. But her boss seemed to have conveniently forgotten this fact. "You told me to wait for you," she said nervously.

"No I didn't." Dominic corrected her.

"But Dominic…" Louise began to argue but her employer shot her down with a cold stare.

"Since you have so much trouble understanding my instructions, I want you to listen very carefully," Dominic said, "because I am going to tell you exactly what I want you to do."

Louise nodded, "Yes, sir."

"I want you to go back to the horse truck, pack your bags and leave."

Louise looked puzzled. "What? You're joking, right?"

"Blackwell doesn't joke!" Dominic replied. "Get your stuff together and go! As of this moment, you no longer work for me. I don't need some half-witted incompetent as my head girl."

Louise was horrified.

"Now get out of my sight!" Dominic roared. "You're fired."

He turned to his junior groom. "Oh and Frannie? You can go too."

Frannie stood there for a moment in disbelief. "Me? But why?"

"Because," Dominic said through gritted teeth, "I was in the middle of a very important conversation with one of my owners when you interrupted me!"

"But you would have missed your ride if I hadn't come to get you!" Frannie blurted out.

"Talking back counts as insubordination in my stables!" Dominic snapped. "You are double-fired!"

As the realisation dawned that her boss was serious, Frannie promptly burst into tears and followed Louise who was already stomping off to the horse truck.

Dominic Blackwell watched their departure with a smug sense of satisfaction. After a disappointing performance in the arena it had at least cheered him up to rage at his staff. It was of slight concern that he'd fired both girls at once. Normally Dominic liked to keep at least one groom in his good books but his temper had been taking its toll lately. He'd fired six grooms in the past six months and these two raised the total to eight.

Dominic Blackwell frowned. He should have held his temper until Frannie had finished her work and then fired her. Now he would be forced to untack Maxi himself. Some riders enjoyed being around their horses; schooling and training – but Dominic Blackwell was not one of them. He lived purely for the thrill of the show ring and the roar of the adoring crowd. The behind-the-scenes stuff was what grooms were for. Or, he thought, that was what they had been for before he got rid of them all.

The problem was, Dominic had developed a bit of a reputation on the circuit and good staff were becoming harder and harder for him to find.

Well, big deal. Dominic huffed as he unsaddled Maxi and loaded his own kit into the truck. Grooms were a dime a dozen. There was bound to be a good, keen stablehand out there who'd be thrilled to work for the famous Dominic Blackwell – a professional head girl who could meet his exacting and high standards without falling apart. The perfect groom was out there. He just had to find her.

Georgie Parker stood up her stirrups and looked directly between the pair of ears in front of her, fixing her gaze on the hedge.

It was hardly a big fence, not by Blainford Academy standards, and Georgie didn't even bother to slow Belladonna down as she came at it. She let the mare gallop, only taking a last-minute check on the reins when she was close enough to see a stride and then sitting deep in the saddle and driving the mare on with her legs. The mare's dark bay ears pricked forward at the hedge and then Georgie felt the horse lift up beneath her. There was that brilliant moment of suspension when they were sailing in mid-air, and then they were landing again on the other side and galloping for home.

The grounds of the school were in sight and ahead of them was the start of the bridle path that led to the school grounds. This was the route the students usually took to the stables, but instead Georgie veered sharply to the right, urging Belle to stay in a gallop as she rode the mare in a straight line towards the stable block over the open grazing fields of the Academy.

"It's OK," she told the mare as she leaned down low over her neck, "we're going off-road. This is a shortcut."

Belle's gallop stretched out, her strides devouring the green pasture. Georgie perched up in her stirrups, her weight in her heels to keep balance, her eyes still trained directly between the mare's ears. Ahead of her she could see the fence that ran around the perimeter of the stables. Like most of the fences in Lexington Kentucky it was an elegant post and plank fence, with a five-bar wooden gate at the entrance near the stables. It would be easy enough for Georgie to pull Belle up and get off and open the gate – but where was the fun in that?

As they neared the gate, Belle snorted and hung back. She knew the difference between a jump and a school gate and she wasn't sure about hurdling the obstacle in front of her. But Georgie put her legs on firmly and urged the mare with her voice and Belle surged forward, putting in one-two-three neat strides before soaring the five-bar gate as if it were no more than a cavaletti.

They arced over the gate, landing neatly on the grass on the other side, and by the time they had reached the verge of the concrete forecourt Georgie had pulled the mare up to a walk and was dismounting.

"Good girl!" Georgie gave the mare a slappy pat on the neck. She had run her stirrups up and was leading the mare towards the stalls when she caught sight of the boy in prefect uniform rounding the corner of the stable block.

"Uh-oh," Georgie groaned as she recognised the

arrogant lope and russet hair of Burghley's head prefect, Conrad Miller.

Georgie could tell by the smirk on Conrad's face that he'd seen her take the shortcut over the gate.

"Hey, Parker!" His voice had the officious tone of a parking warden. "Students aren't allowed to jump school fences; it's against Blainford rules."

Georgie felt a sudden sting of anger. Ever since she'd arrived at the Academy Conrad had taken a perverse joy in picking on her. Last term things had come to a head when Georgie's boyfriend Riley had held a mallet to Conrad's throat at the school polo tournament, publicly telling him to back off and leave Georgie alone. For the rest of the term Conrad had heeded Riley's warning, but clearly he had now decided that the truce was about to come to an end.

"You've got Fatigues, Parker!" Conrad said.

Georgie gave the prefect a withering look. "You're a real numnah, Conrad."

"Watch your attitude, Parker – or you'll be on Double Fatigues." Conrad shot back.

Georgie groaned. There was no point in arguing with

Conrad. Besides, it would take more than Fatigues to dent her spirits. Tomorrow was the first day of the new term at Blainford and Georgie was back with a vengeance.

Last term she had been dropped from Tara Kelly's cross-country class and had to play polo instead. But now her dreams of eventing glory were back on track – she had regained her coveted place in the class for the last term of the year. And while she still had numnahs like Conrad to deal with – and even worse, his spoilt princess of a girlfriend, Kennedy Kirkwood, trying to take her down – she didn't care.

The past few months riding polo ponies had made Georgie fearless. Her riding had improved and her bond with Belle was stronger than ever. She trusted the mare completely – and more importantly, Belle trusted Georgie. They would be unstoppable on the cross-country course. Which was just as well because apparently this term Tara Kelly had a real test in store for them.

Georgie had heard the murmurings around the school ever since she had returned from her holidays. The final term exam would wind up eliminating more than one member of the cross-country class. By the time the year was over, only a handful of the Academy's elite young riders from around the world would remain – and Georgie was determined that she would be one of them.

Chapter Two

*G*eorgie Parker was one of the lucky ones – unlike some girls who have to beg and plead their parents for a pony, she was born into a horsey family, destined to ride.

When Georgie joined her local pony club there were whispers that she had an unfair advantage, having a famous, world-class eventing rider for a mother. In reality, Georgie's mum, Ginny Parker, was extremely busy with her string of eventers so her daughter had to look after her own pony. And as for spoiling her with pricey show ponies, Mrs Parker insisted that good looks and glamour were the last things that mattered in a horse. Georgie's first two ponies, Smokey and Millie, wouldn't have won any beauty contests, but they were bombproof and sweet-natured.

Georgie was ten years old when her mum bought her Tyro. The black Connemara was barely broken-in when they brought him home to their farm in Little Brampton.

"You'll school him yourself," Ginny Parker told her daughter firmly. "It won't be easy, but it will make you a better rider. And one day he'll be a brilliant pony and you'll be able to say that you taught him everything he knows."

Bringing on a green pony like Tyro wasn't easy, but Georgie worked hard over the winter months so that when spring came she was ready to take him out to his first competition.

Unfortunately, the Little Brampton gymkhana dates clashed with the Blenheim three-star horse trials. Georgie usually accompanied her mum to all the big events as her junior groom, but she was so desperate to give Tyro his first outing she decided to go to the gymkhana instead. Her mum's best friend, Lucinda Milwood, who ran the local riding school, would accompany her.

Georgie would always look back on her decision that day with regret. But how could she have known that while she was having the time of her life at the local gymkhana, events at Blenheim were about to change her life forever.

Georgie still remembered the devastation on her father's face when she had walked in with her armful of red ribbons. "Where's Mum? Isn't she back yet?"

Then her father's words, chilling and ominous. "Georgie… There's been an accident, your mother fell on the cross-country course…"

Her mother's death devastated Georgie, but there was a second blow to come. Grieving for his wife, Georgie's dad, Dr Parker, could no longer face being surrounded by her horses. So he sold off Ginny's eventers, and would have got rid of Tyro too if Lucinda Milwood hadn't offered to keep the pony at her riding school.

In exchange for Tyro's livery, Georgie helped Lucinda around the stables. The yard became like a second home to her over the next three years. Despite her mother's tragic accident, Georgie was determined to follow in her footsteps and become an international eventer, and with Lucinda's support she finally convinced her father to let her audition for Blainford Academy.

Blainford, the exclusive equestrian boarding school in Kentucky, USA, had a track record for producing world champions in every field of horse sports. Georgie's mum and Lucinda had both been pupils there, and it was Georgie's dream to take her pony and go there too.

But when Georgie aced the auditions Dr Parker broke the news that he couldn't afford to send Tyro with her. The fees for the Academy were exorbitant for Georgie alone, and the cost of shipping her beloved Connemara all the way from the UK to the USA – plus the boarding fees for the pony – would simply be too much.

Desperate to go Blainford, Georgie was forced to make one of the toughest decisions of her young life. She agreed to sell Tyro and ride one of the Blainford school horses instead.

That horse turned out to be Belladonna. Beautiful, talented, and oh-so-difficult, the bay mare with the white heart on her forehead had something special about her. It wasn't until halfway through the first term that Georgie found out that she had been paired her up with the foal of Ginny Parker's favourite mare, Boudicca.

Belle was a complicated ride and Georgie had spent

the first three terms at Blainford coming to grips with this difficult new horse.

Then, just when she was finally connecting with Belle, came the worst blow of all. Georgie was dropped from cross-country class.

Faced with finding a new riding subject, Georgie had taken up polo. Belle coped surprisingly well with the fast-paced, rough action on the polo field, despite being sixteen hands high when most polo ponies were fifteen-two. But Georgie knew that the mare's special abilities were wasted on chasing a little white ball. Belladonna was bred to jump – plus she had the speed and stamina required to make a great eventing horse. Their comeback in Tara's class this term wasn't just about Georgie – it was a chance for Belle to prove herself too.

The boarders had been trickling back into Blainford all that weekend, returning in time for the start of the new term on Monday. Georgie's room mate, Alice Dupree, came with the news that she was no longer riding her beloved William. She had brought back a new horse on the truck from Maryland and the Badminton House girls couldn't wait to get down to the stables to meet him.

"Don't get too excited," Alice told them as they walked along the driveway to the stable block. "He's another hand-me-down – like all of my horses."

Alice inherited horses the way most girls got their big sisters' outgrown clothes. She was the third Dupree sister to attend Blainford. Her eldest sister, Cherry, was now a professional rider on the national showjumping circuit, and Alice's new horse, Caspian, had belonged to her.

"He was supposed to be Cherry's next Grand Prix superstar," Alice told the others, "but Cherry's been crazy-busy with work, riding other people's horses. Mum said since Caspian wasn't getting ridden, Cherry should give him to me for the term."

Until now, Alice had been riding William the Conqueror, a well-bred chestnut warmblood. But over the holidays she had noticed that Will was scratchy on his left foreleg. By the last week of the holiday that scratchiness had developed into a hoof abscess and Will was lame. When the vet was called out to the Dupree ranch to cut out the abscess he did some x-rays and found that the gelding also had degenerative arthritis in his hocks. The abscess would cure – but the hocks were a disaster. It was the end of William's jumping career.

The Badminton House girls knew how much Alice had adored Will. But she seemed pretty thrilled with having Caspian as his replacement – and when they arrived at the stables they could see why.

Caspian was a stunner. A long-limbed Oldenburg, pale grey with dapples on his shoulders and rump, and a steel-grey mane and tail, he stood in his loose box and nibbled blithely on his hay net while the girls admired his beauty.

"He's gorgeous!" Emily was wide-eyed.

"I know!" Alice looked at him possessively. "He's so handsome I just keep staring at him!"

"Is he any good at cross-country?" Daisy asked.

"He's never done it," Alice conceded. "He's brilliant over coloured poles, but that's all he's ever jumped with Cherry. I guess I'll find out tomorrow."

Monday afternoon would be when the eventers had their lesson with Tara Kelly.

"Tara might take it easy on us," Emily Tait said hopefully. "It's only our first day back."

Daisy gave a hollow laugh. "I doubt it!"

Emily turned to Georgie. "Can she eliminate you a second time? Or do you have immunity now?"

Alice frowned. "It's not an episode of *Survivor*, Emily. No one gets 'immunity'!" She did air quotes as she said the last bit.

Georgie agreed. "Just because Tara let me back into the class doesn't mean she won't get rid of me again."

"Someone's going to have to go," Daisy said bluntly. "We won't all make it through to the second year."

"Can we not talk about this?" Emily said, getting upset. "I don't want to lose any of my friends."

"Geez, Emily, it's only getting kicked out of cross-country class," Daisy told her. "It's not like life and death!"

"Isn't it?" Alice questioned.

All the girls knew that at Blainford, where the cliques ruled the school, being Tara Kelly's eventers was like a badge that you wore with pride. While the polo boys were rich and arrogant, the showjumperettes were glamorous and stuck-up, the westerns were laidback and the dressage geeks intense and uptight, the eventers stood out as fearless and loyal.

Apart from Kennedy and Arden, who had transferred from showjumping and had always made it quite clear that they wanted nothing to do with their classmates, Tara Kelly's first-years were a tight-knit bunch.

The danger that they faced on the cross-country course gave them a sense of camaraderie. But there was also a fierce rivalry amongst them for class rankings. Tara Kelly went through her ruthless elimination cull of her pupils in the first year to make sure that only the very best were allowed to continue up the grades. The way Tara saw it, elimination wasn't about ruining young lives, it was about saving them.

Eventing was a demanding subject – and a deadly one for any rider who wasn't skilled enough to meet the challenge. Travelling at a fast gallop over solid fences meant huge risks for both horse and rider. Even the rodeo class had a grudging respect for the broken bone count in the eventing department. Incredibly, so far the first-year eventing class had avoided any major injuries.

Or at least they had done until now. As they left the stables and walked up the school driveway the girls spied Nicholas Laurent ahead of them. The French rider was one of their cross-country gang and he was on crutches and sporting a bright blue plaster cast on his leg that went all the way to the knee.

By the time the girls reached the dining hall, Nicholas was already in the queue, trying to hold his dinner tray whilst balancing on a single crutch. The other eventing boys – Cameron Fraser, Alex Chang and Matt Garrett – were all with him but none of them were offering to help. Instead, they were greedily dishing burgers and fries on to their own plates.

"Don't you guys ever think about anyone else?" Alice said casting a dark look at Cameron and the others as she stepped forward to relieve the grateful Nicholas of his tray. "Nicholas, you go and sit down. I'll get your food and bring it over for you."

"Merci, Alice," Nicholas said. "Get me extra frites, OK?" He hobbled off to take a seat at the eventers' usual table while Alice piled his plate and her own. As soon as Laurent's back was turned the girls began whispered speculations on the cause of the broken leg.

"Do you think he did it practising cross-country?" Emily asked.

Georgie shook her head. "I bet he did it on the hunt field in Bordeaux."

"I hope the horse was OK," Alice said looking back over her shoulder at him as she dished up the fries. "It looks like it must have been a bad fall."

When the girls finally joined Nicholas and the other boys at the table, however, he refused to tell them anything about the accident.

"I don't want to talk about it," Nicholas was adamant.

"Why not?" Matt Garrett frowned.

"Because…" Nicholas paused. "Because… it is no big deal. There is nothing to say."

"Nicholas," Alice was insistent, "you're in a cast. You have crutches. It looks like a big deal to us."

Nicholas shrugged.

"Come on," Cameron persisted. "Tell us how you did it."

Nicholas cast a sideways glance, checking the room to see if anyone else was near the eventers' table.

"OK," he said, leaning in over the table, his voice hushed in a conspiratorial tone. "I will tell you what happened."

The riders all leaned in and waited in silence for him to speak. Nicholas looked serious. And then, in a quiet voice he said, "I was playing tennis."

There was a choking sound as Matt Garrett almost snorted his orange juice out through his nose. "Tennis? Seriously? You did it playing tennis?"

Nicholas looked around the room nervously. "Please don't tell anyone," he said. "I've already had three girls ask to sign my cast. They think I did it falling off on a three-star course in Saumur. If they knew that I tripped making a backhand shot it wouldn't be good for my reputation."

The whole eventing table were laughing.

"It's not funny," Nicholas said indignantly. "It's a hairline fracture at the ankle. I'll be in this cast for seven weeks."

"You've got to see the irony, Nicholas," Alice said.

"You've survived three terms in Tara's class and then you go home for two weeks and manage to break a leg playing tennis!"

"Shhh!" Nicholas hushed her. "Someone will hear you."

"Bad luck, mate," Matt Garrett drawled in his heavy Australian accent. "I suppose this means you're eliminated since you can't ride?"

Nicholas glared at him. "No, actually. Tara's offered me a place in the second year already based on my class ranking."

"Is that so?" Matt looked less than impressed with this news. "Smart move, man – instant upgrade without any final exam pressure. Maybe I should have broken my leg too."

"There's plenty of time for that," Nicholas shot back.

"I don't think so, Nico," Matt replied, turning back to his burger. "I don't fall off."

"If you were handing out a prize for arrogance how could you choose between Nicholas and Matt?" Alice said as they walked to class the next morning.

"I feel sorry for Nicholas," Emily said. "It must be awful not being able to ride."

"Totally," Georgie agreed. "Tough as Tara's classes are, it's even worse when you're not in them."

Today, at last, Georgie was returning to cross-country class. But first she had regular morning school lessons to get through.

Blainford Academy split the school day into two halves. The morning classes were held in the main grounds of the college in the red brick Georgian buildings that surrounded the green square of grass in the middle of the school known as the quad.

Mornings were taken up with science and maths, French and German, geography and English – during which the Blainford girls dressed like students at any other exclusive private school, in blue pleated pinafore dresses and navy blazers with the school crest in pale blue and silver on the breast pocket.

But after lunch the pupils headed back to their boarding houses and changed into their 'number twos' – their riding uniform of navy jods and a pale blue shirt – in preparation for their afternoon lessons with their horses.

For Tara Kelly's class the pupils were also required to wear back protectors, and as Georgie did up the Velcro straps on hers that afternoon she felt like her old self once more: back in the eventers' ranks, where she belonged.

In the loose box beside her, Belle was tacked up and ready to go in her cross-country saddle and martingale. Georgie was bent down adjusting the tendon boots on the mare's forelegs when she caught sight of someone leaning over the Dutch door. Georgie looked up expecting to see one of her classmates. Her smile evaporated when she caught sight of the glossy red hair and waspish features of Kennedy Kirkwood.

"So it's true that you're making a comeback?" Kennedy's tone was sarky. "What a pity. I'd hoped it was just a vicious rumour."

Georgie stood up and wiped her hands on her jods. "Yeah," she said, "tough luck, Kennedy. And after you went to all that trouble of sabotaging me."

"Wow!" Kennedy put her manicured hands to her face in mock horror. "That really hurts, Georgie. You know, it's such a shame the way things have turned out with us."

"Yeah," Georgie agreed. "You're right Kennedy. Where did things go wrong? Do you think it was when you tried to split up me and James by writing fake letters or when you nearly killed me by barging into my horse on the cross-country course?"

"Oh, poor Georgie!" Kennedy sighed. "It's always someone else's fault, isn't it? You're always looking for someone to blame for your failures. Playing for sympathy because you've got no breeding, no money, no talent and no mommy."

Georgie was speechless. Even by Kirkwood standards it was vicious.

Kennedy looked Georgie right in the eye, her voice as cold as steel. "You've been a thorn in my side ever since you got to this school. I've watched my lame brother fall for your British act like he's Prince William and you're Kate Middleton. And I've watched Tara treat you like you're something special. But the truth is you don't deserve to be at Blainford. You think the past three terms have been tough, Parker? You've got no idea how miserable I can make your wormy little life."

"Is that a threat?" Georgie asked in disbelief.

"Duh!" Kennedy pulled a face. "I'm a Kirkwood. We don't make threats. We have staff to do that stuff for us."

Smirking, Kennedy turned to leave and then swung back around. "By the way, my boyfriend asked me to remind you you're on Fatigues this week. He hasn't forgotten, and he's got something special planned, just for you."

Chapter Three

Typical Kennedy, Georgie fumed as she led Belle out of her box, *she waits until now to confront me so that she'll throw me off my game right before Tara's class.*

She knew Kennedy well enough to recognise her transparent tactics, but that didn't make it any easier to calm down. She was still bristling with latent fury as she rode towards her classmates who were already assembling on the cross-country course.

"What's up with you?" Alice asked when saw the look on Georgie's face.

"Kennedy is what's up," Georgie hissed. She could see the showjumperettes watching and she didn't want to give Kennedy the satisfaction of knowing they were talking about her. "She's a total witch!"

"And this is news how?" Alice muttered back. "Georgie, you know she only has it in for you because she thinks you're a threat..."

The students suddenly fell silent as a young woman wearing dove grey jodhpurs and a crisp white blouse walked to the front leading a bay gelding. Her demeanour made it clear that she was in charge.

"Welcome back," Tara Kelly said. "I know your horses are fresh from having two weeks' holiday, and Alice has a new horse who has never done cross-country before, so we are going to spend the day doing confidence-building exercises."

The eventing mistress mounted up on the handsome bright bay, which Georgie now recognised as Lagerfeld, Nicholas Laurent's well-bred Selle Francais. Tara was keeping the horse in work while Nicholas was in plaster.

"Our basics today consist of three classic 'bogey' fences," Tara said, "and the twist is, we're going to be jumping them at a walk."

Daisy looked at the ditch that Tara had nominated as their first fence. "She can't be serious!"

Alex Chang raised a tentative hand.

"Yes, Alex?"

"I don't get it," Alex said. "We're never going to walk over jumps in a real-life cross-country, are we?"

"No," Tara agreed. "But there are many things that we do when we are schooling that we wouldn't do in actual competition. Can anyone tell me what the benefits are of schooling over jumps at a walk?"

"It's slower?" Emily said.

The others sniggered but Tara confirmed that she was right, "Exactly! The slower the pace that you come at a fence, the more time you have to think and react. Any other reasons?"

No one else raised a hand. "Keeping our horses in a walk allows them to stay cool and calm," Tara said. "It gives them a chance to negotiate the fence. Remember, it's the horse's job to get over it, not yours! They must learn to be clever jumpers."

Tara walked Lagerfeld over towards the first jump, a narrow ditch.

"It's not a big ditch," Tara said. She adjusted her reins to prepare the gelding. "I'm going to let Lagerfeld take a good look as he approaches it."

Lagerfeld walked forward until he was just a couple of metres in front of the fence. Then the big bay suddenly realised that there was a channel in the ground ahead of him and with a stricken snort he tried to back off. Tara kept calm her legs firmly on at his sides. Lagerfeld lowered his head so that he could get a really good look, with his nose almost down in the ditch and then with a grunt he took one more step and then vaulted it with an ungainly deer leap. Tara stayed with him in the saddle and pulled him up neatly on the other side of the ditch.

"Good boy!" Tara said giving the big bay a slappy pat on his glossy neck.

"As you can see, the key is to let them look but keep them moving forward. Right! Mr Fraser, I think we'll have you over it next. No jogging, no trotting and absolutely no cantering. And on no account do we ever turn them away or let them refuse!"

One by one, the riders took their turns walking over the ditch. When the time came for Caspian's turn he seemed quite spooked by the jump, giving guttural snorts that sounded like a steam train being channelled through his nostrils.

"Don't turn him away, Alice!" Tara was firm. "Back him up three strides and then push him forward again!"

Alice did as she was told, and with much dramatic snorting and fretting Caspian took three steps and popped over the ditch.

"Excellent! Make a fuss of him!" Tara called out.

The water jump was next. The horses had to step off a ledge less than half a metre high and into the pond below. Again, the novice Caspian snorted and fussed on the water's edge. "Keep him moving forward, that's it!" Tara encouraged as Alice urged the horse with a brisk bounce of her heels against his sides.

Surprisingly, some of the other riders with more experienced horses also had trouble at the water. When Cameron and Paddy stopped dead on the edge of the pond and the big piebald dithered on the bank Tara wasn't very impressed

"Come on, Mr Fraser!" she commanded. "If you can't get your horse to walk through this little puddle then how on earth do you expect it to leap into the lake at the Burghley Horse Trials?"

The last fence the horses had to tackle was a downhill

staircase, a series of three low steps cut into a bank, each with a stride between them. Tara encouraged the riders to walk their horses down the tiers on a loose rein. When Matt Garrett's horse, a handsome dun called Tigerland, managed to lose his footing and trip down a step, Tara praised Matt for staying still in the saddle and letting the horse find his feet again.

"That's right!" Tara said, "Give him a pat. Making mistakes like that is natural – that's how they learn."

Georgie had thought that walking Belle over obstacles would be a bit dull, but this was a trust-building exercise and the mare seemed to blossom as she tackled the jumps with Georgie's gentle support. Belle took it all in her stride, negotiating the ditch with a graceful leap. The mare splashed about happily in the water jump, pawing at the water so keenly that Georgie worried for a moment that she might actually try to drop down to her knees and roll for the sheer fun of it. At the staircase, the riders had only had one chance to tackle the jump when Tara called it a day.

"We'll have to leave it at that I'm afraid," Tara told the class. "There's an assembly for first-year pupils this afternoon. Can you all take your horses back to the stables and then meet me at the indoor arena in fifteen minutes, please?"

"What's this about?" Daisy demanded as the girls headed for the indoor arena. "We're missing a whole hour of class."

"I don't get why we're going to the indoor arena," Emily said. "If it's school notices or something Tara could have just told us out on the cross-country course."

As they entered the arena the girls noticed other first years also arriving. Georgie spotted dressage riders Mitty Janssen and Isabel Weiss already seated with their classmates in the tiered seats facing the sawdust arena.

"The Westerns are here too," Alice noted as she spied Tyler McGuane and Bunny Redpath making their way up the stairs to sit with Jenner Philips and Blair Danner.

The eventers were nearly the last ones in so they sat in the front two rows. Georgie, Alice, Daisy and Emily crammed into the end seats of the second row right behind Alex and Cam.

Cam was looking worried. "What if they're going to spring a test on us?" he fretted. "I haven't studied!"

Alice sighed. "It's our first day back, Cam. None of us have studied."

The last students to arrive were Kennedy and Arden. They made a pointed display of sitting as far away as possible from Georgie and the Badminton girls.

Suddenly the overhead lights in the rig above the arena popped and crackled into life, casting a white glare over the sand. Voices could be heard in the wings of the main entrance and a moment later Tara Kelly strode in accompanied by three other members of the Blainford teaching staff – dressage teacher Bettina Schmidt, showjumping master Trent Chase, and Hank 'Shep' Shepard, the head of the Western faculty.

Walking alongside them wearing stiff brown tweed was Mrs Dickins-Thomson, Blainford's headmistress.

If she were a horse, Mrs Dickins-Thomson would have been a rangy Thoroughbred. Her long face was dominated by a Roman nose and a mane of chestnut hair. Formidable and stern, the headmistress possessed a commanding presence – and the first-year students fell respectfully silent as she cleared her throat to speak.

"For many years now Blainford Academy has built a reputation as the premier equestrian institute in the world. Our pupils go on to become world champions in every field. But to maintain that status we must move with the times and adapt. We have to ensure that the skills that you are learning at the school are directly applicable to the workforce."

Mrs Dickins-Thomson paused. "And that is why, for the first time, we are introducing the new first-year apprentice programme."

The bewildered faces of the young riders stared back at her.

"Hey, does she mean like that TV show with Alan Sugar?" Cameron whispered.

Alice kicked his seat to make him shut up.

"The Blainford apprenticeship programme utilises the resource of former pupils, alumni of the Academy, who have kindly agreed to take a current pupil under their wing," Mrs Dickins-Thomson explained. "You will spend one term as their apprentice and your performance will be assessed as your final exam for the year."

Alice boldly raised her hand. "Do you mean that they're going to be, like, our private instructors?"

Mrs Dickins-Thomson shook her head. "No, Alice, not your instructors. They are your employers. This is not a classroom situation we're putting you into – this is real life. You'll be working as professional grooms. They will treat you exactly as they would their own employees. They have the power to hire or fire you and, since this is the real world, there will be no make-up test and no reprieves…"

Georgie felt as if Mrs Dickins-Thomson was referring specifically to her.

The headmistress clapped her hands briskly together. "Starting from next week you are apprenticed to your new masters. We haven't been able to place all of you within your unique disciplines. However, your apprenticeships will provide you with valuable experience and skills. So no complaints please because there will be no transfers. It goes without saying that I expect all of you to represent your school in the appropriate manner and show our former pupils that Blainford remains the best equestrian academy in the United States."

"For most of you the routine of normal morning classes here at the school will not alter," the headmistress told them. "All afternoon classes will be cancelled so that you can attend your apprenticeships from next week onward. Also, when required, you may be given additional weekend leave to perform your duties as many of these riders will require you on weekends for competitions."

The first-years began chattering excitedly and Mrs Dickins-Thomson raised her hand to demand silence before she spoke again.

"It gives me great pleasure now to introduce you to your new employers." The headmistress turned to face the entrance to the arena. "Former pupils of the Academy, would you please come out into the arena and join us?"

Through the doorway a group of men and women appeared, some of them dressed in jodhpurs, others in jeans, T-shirts and baseball caps, walking in unison towards the headmistress across the sand.

"That woman at the front looks really familiar," Alice frowned as she stared at the woman in the beige jods and yellow jersey.

"Ohmygod!" Emily clapped a hand over her mouth in shock. "It's Tina Dixon! I just saw a photo of her in *Horsing Around Magazine*."

Blonde and tanned, Tina Dixon was engrossed in conversation with a hard-faced woman with short cropped brown hair.

"That's Allegra Hickman talking to her," Alex Chang said. "She's the only American to ever be ranked in the top ten dressage riders in the world."

Beside Allegra, a tall man with honey-coloured hair and a matching tan cast a supercilious glance across the arena.

"Dominic Blackwell," Alice hissed in Georgie's ear. "Cherry has a poster of him on her wall at home. He's a showjumper – he's in the national team."

It was strange, to see these famous riders right here in front of them, talking and laughing with each other. It was becoming clear that every one of the men and women in the arena was an equestrian superstar.

"Right!" Mrs Dickins-Thomson continued. "We're going to do this class by class, beginning with Tara Kelly's eventing pupils."

Tara stepped forward and opened the manila folder in her hands.

"I'm going to call you out one by one to come down to the arena to be introduced to your new employer."

Tara read the first name on her list.

"Emily Tait?"

Emily looked extremely nervous as she stood up and walked down between the seats to the arena. Painfully shy at the best of times, she was almost shaking as she stood in front of the elite riders that were assembled behind Tara Kelly.

"Emily is from New Zealand and she's consistently at the top of my class rankings," Tara did the introductions. "Emily, I am pairing you with Tina Dixon. Tina, as you are all no doubt aware, recently came third at the Lexington Four-star event and has made the US eventing development squad."

Tina Dixon stepped forward, waved to the class and thrust out a tanned and sinewy arm to shake hands with Emily. "I've already got a New Zealander grooming for me so you'll fit right in with my team," she informed her. "Welcome aboard."

"Alice Dupree?" Tara called the next name on the list.

Alice looked more excited than daunted as she took her turn to join the superstars in the arena.

"Alice is from Maryland where her family breeds eventers and showjumpers," Tara told the assembled riders. "Jumping is her strength, but her dressage needs work so that's why I'm assigning her to you, Allegra."

The excited smile on Alice's face slipped. She was being assigned to Allegra Hickman – a dressage rider!

If Tara noticed the look of disappointment on Alice's face she didn't acknowledge it.

"Allegra's achievements include a gold medal at the games in Saumur for her musical dressage performance in the kur," she read the notes in her folder to the class. "She currently has two Grand Prix mounts and four horses in her stables at Prix St Georges level and is a great supporter of the modern dressage method."

Allegra stepped forward and gave a stiff wave to the students, then shook Alice's hand and stepped back into the ranks of the riders, taking Alice with her.

"Cameron Fraser?" Tara called out.

Tara consulted her notes. "Cameron, I am pairing you up with Frank Carsey. Frank, where are you?"

There was a general murmur as everyone looked around expectantly for Frank Carsey. Then a small hand appeared, poking up from behind the riders and waving to make its presence known.

"Make way! Coming through."

Frank was lithe and wiry with pointy features and slicked-back brown hair. But the truly notable thing about his appearance was his height – or rather lack of it. Frank Carsey was a jockey and he was tiny. When Cam stepped forward to shake his hand he towered over him by a whole head.

"Last year Frank Carsey won more division one races than any other jockey in the state of Kentucky," Tara said. "He has a reputation for turning horses around and if you want to learn how to condition a horse and get it into peak galloping performance for eventing then Frank is your man."

"You're a bit taller than I'd hoped," the diminutive jockey told his new apprentice, "but you're light enough to ride trackwork. See you at the yards at four am on Monday."

"Four am?" Cam squeaked.

Tara confirmed this. "Some of you will be working early mornings as well as afternoons to keep to the timetables of your employers."

"Daisy King?" Tara called out the next name on her list and Daisy rose from her seat. "Here!"

Daisy and Georgie had known each other back in the UK, but they were never friends back then. Daisy had always been far too competitive to make friends. At Blainford, however, the girls had been thrust together in the same boarding house and Georgie had developed a grudging admiration for Daisy's single-minded will to win. While that made it hard sometimes to be her friend, it also meant that Daisy was someone you wanted on your team.

"Daisy King has been eventing since she was eleven," Tara introduced her. "She won the national UK secondary schools ODE finals last year."

Tara paused. "Last term Daisy was on the girls' polo team that won the low-goal award at the Bluegrass Cup.

And I think her natural abilities as an all-round rider could further benefit from more polo training which is why I have assigned her to you, Sebastian."

A man stepped forward from the ranks of the elite trainers. He was devastatingly handsome, in a broad-shouldered and unshaven way. He had jet black hair and startling blue eyes and he wore the number three jersey for his polo team, along with the regulation uniform of polo whites and long brown boots.

"Seb Upton-Baker is an eight-goal player," Tara smiled at him. "We've been friends since school – and we're very lucky that he divides his time between his polo ranch in Argentina, his polo club in London and his small holding here in Kentucky. Seb will be playing this season on a patron team and Daisy is grooming for him."

Daisy didn't notice the envious looks that she was getting from Kennedy and Arden. In fact, she was a bit miffed about being lumbered with the hunky polo player when all she'd really wanted was to work on Tina Dixon's yard.

Georgie, meanwhile, was on the edge of her seat. With

all of her friends already allocated their apprenticeships, she was expecting Tara to call her name next. But instead, Tara worked her way through allocating apprenticeships to every other member of the class. Georgie watched as both Alex and Matt were placed in well-respected Kentucky eventing stables and Arden was put in the hands of a woman named Frisky Newton who ran a famous breaking-in facility for green horses. Even Nicholas Laurent was given a placement at the Bloodstock association offices which ran the Thoroughbred breeding programme.

In the end, only Kennedy and Georgie were left.

"Kennedy Kirkwood and Georgina Parker," Tara called both their names at once. Georgie had to walk down the stairs with Kennedy so that they were both standing with their eventing teacher in the arena.

"Kennedy comes from the famous Kirkwood showjumping family, and was a showjumper herself before she swapped codes to join the eventing class," Tara told the assembled riders.

"And Georgie was in the House Team that won the showjumping cup earlier this year…" Tara said.

"So it seemed logical that you should both be placed with Dominic Blackwell. Dominic, as you all know, is a member of the US showjumping team. He has been kind enough to offer to take two apprentices at his stables."

Instead of shaking hands with his new apprentices like the other riders had done Dominic Blackwell walked over to Georgie and stuck his palm up in mid-air.

"Hey! Team Blackwell! High-five!"

Georgie stared back blankly, leaving Dominic Blackwell holding his hand aloft.

"C'mon!" Dominic Blackwell was undeterred. His enthusiasm amped up even higher. "You'll be working at the best showjumping stables in the whole of the Southern States! Can I get a high-five?"

"Woo! Yeah!" It was Kennedy, doing a peppy little cheerleader skip and barging roughly past Georgie. She made a lunge at Dominic Blackwell and slapped a high-five on his open palm. Then she gave him a perky grin. "Go Team Blackwell!" she cheered brightly.

"Yess!" Dominic grinned like a maniac. He turned to Georgie once more. "C'mon, Julie," he said, getting Georgie's name wrong. "Give me some skin!"

Georgie rolled her eyes but clearly Dominic was not giving up. She stepped forward and slapped the palm of her hand hard against Dominic Blackwell's.

"Woo! Welcome aboard, Julie! Go Team Blackwell!"

And Georgie knew that she was about to spend the next term in hell.

Chapter Four

The track at Keeneland Park was shrouded in fog at five in the morning. Georgie stood at the railing and watched Riley and Marco galloping into the mist, until they disappeared completely at the third furlong. She peered into the gloom, listening to the rhythmic pounding of Marco's hooves, the beat growing ever more distant and then coming closer as Riley and the horse emerged once more.

Georgie marvelled at the feline grace of the golden Thoroughbred and the skill of the boy on his back. As they turned the corner of the track and came down the home straight in front of the grandstand Riley began to urge the gelding on, pumping his arms above the horse's neck and suddenly the hoof beats began to quicken.

The chestnut gelding was responding to his jockey, extending his stride so that his body seemed to flatten out and devour the ground as he thundered down the track.

She was so lost in the beauty of the spectacle that Georgie almost forgot to press the stopwatch as the gelding's nose reached the line.

With an emphatic click, she hit the button. Then she checked the time, popped it back in her pocket and waited for Riley. He had eased Marco down to a canter and then a trot and had carried on around the track to cool the Thoroughbred down before he came over to the railing to join her.

"So?" Riley looked at her expectantly. "How did he do?"

"He covered eight furlongs in one minute forty-one," Georgie said.

Riley looked pleased and gave Marco a slappy pat. "Hey, not bad, boy!" he told the chestnut.

"Is that time good enough to win the Firecracker?" Georgie asked.

"Maybe," Riley said, "but there's a big difference

between blowing him out like this on the track all alone and riding a real race when sixteen other jockeys are trying to cut in front or ram you off the track. It's not until you're coming down that final furlong with the pack at your heels that you find out what your horse is really made of."

Georgie looked at the little chestnut gelding dancing and fretting anxiously beneath Riley. Less than six months ago if you had asked any racing pundit in the country whether this scrawny, diminutive horse stood a chance of winning the coveted Firecracker Handicap, a race worth $232,000 in prize money, they would have laughed at you. Marco's racing career was all but washed up when Georgie purchased him for $150 from his former trainer Tommy Doyle. The dirt cheap price tag reflected the total failure on Marco's part to win any races – and the fact that the four-year old Thoroughbred had a reputation for doing lethal 180 degree turns in the middle of the track which meant that even the bravest jockeys refused to get on him.

Georgie had bought Marco in the hope that she might be able to put his turning tendencies to good use and train him as a polo pony. But Marco was even more lethal on the polo field than he was on the racetrack and Georgie didn't have a clue what to do with him – until Riley had offered to swap him for a more suitable polo mare.

At the time, Georgie's boyfriend was doing her a favour. But it had never occurred to her that Riley could actually see any potential in this difficult and temperamental Thoroughbred. Everyone else had given up on Marco, but Riley persevered with the little chestnut, retraining the horse, experimenting with his feeding and workout schedule, and making friends with the complicated little gelding.

Then, last month, he entered Marco in his first race and the chestnut won by a clear two lengths with Riley on his back.

Looking back, Georgie wasn't surprised that Riley had turned Marco around. Her boyfriend had a way of getting a song out of the most difficult horses. Sometimes Georgie could swear that he had the ability to read their minds. How else could you explain the change in Marco?

"The talented horses are always temperamental," Riley told Georgie. "Marco just needed someone to believe in him."

Riley's belief in Marco was proven justified when the horse won again in his second race. This time the win was hard-fought. Riley had been boxed in behind a clutch of riders on the railing all the way to the three-quarter marker. Things had looked impossible but somehow he had found a hole and driven the chestnut hard towards it to break free of the pack, putting on a burst of speed in the home straight to edge out in front of the favourite by a nose.

Even with two wins under their belt, Riley wasn't content.

"He's still holding back. There's more speed in him," Riley told Georgie as they walked together back to the stables. "Look at him! He's hardly even breathing hard."

Jogging and skipping alongside Riley, Marco was bounding about as if the track beneath his feet were made of hot coals. Riley didn't pay any attention to the Thoroughbred's dangerous antics and eventually Marco stopped larking about and settled down. By the time they had reached the stables he was walking sedately at his jockey's side.

That was the way it was with Riley and horses, Georgie mused. He was real quiet with them, but somehow he always got them to do exactly as he wanted. She had seen that from the moment she met him. She'd been having trouble with Belle in her first term at Blainford and it was Kenny, the Academy's caretaker, who suggested that she get some help from his nephew.

Georgie had been expecting some wizened guy like The Horse Whisperer but it turned out that Riley was a teenager just like her. Riley's dad, John Conway, was the owner of Clemency Farm and Riley worked for him riding track most mornings before his classes at the local High School.

Riley and Georgie had been dating for a term now – despite predictions of doom from Daisy who said it was plain crazy even trying to go out with a boy who didn't attend Blainford. Georgie knew that Riley had his own reservations about dating a girl from a private equestrian school. It didn't help that total numnahs like Conrad were determined to cause trouble. The last time

Riley had clashed with Conrad, the Burghley House head prefect found himself pinned to the wall with a polo mallet at his throat. Georgie hadn't asked Riley back to a school event since then. And she was hardly going to tell him about the fatigues that the prefect had given her last week.

Riley led the gelding into his loose box back at the stable block, and Georgie bolted the door after him.

"Did I tell you that I'm going to enter him in the Hanley Stakes?" Riley asked. "I figure he needs one more outing before the Firecracker, just to keep him on form."

"What sort of race is it?" Georgie asked as she undid Marco's girth.

"A grade three, over a mile and a half," Riley told her as he slipped the gelding's bridle off. "It's a big distance for him, but I want to see how he handles it. He'll be up against The Rainmaker."

Georgie had heard of The Rainmaker. *Thoroughbred Magazine* had called the jet-black stallion "one of the most perfectly put together Thoroughbreds the sport of racing has ever seen" and the smart money was on the big black horse to win at Churchill Downs. At sixteen-three hands high, The Rainmaker was a massive horse compared to Marco who stood at a mere fifteen-two.

Georgie slid the saddle pad off Marco's back, and nearly collapsed under its weight. "Ohmygod!"

"Are you OK?" Riley rushed to take the saddle from her. "Be careful. It's heavy."

How could such a tiny jockey's saddle weigh so much? Georgie stuck her hands into one of the pockets stitched into the brown leather and pulled out a round metal disc.

"What are these?"

"Lead weights," Riley said. "All horses have to carry a certain weight when they run. It's a handicap to even out the odds."

"So will Marco have to carry weights when you race him in the Firecracker?"

"Nah," Riley pulled two more weights out of the lead pad. "I'm already heavier than most of the other jockeys anyway. And Marco and me aren't the favourites by any stretch. But all the same, I've been training him to carry the maximum – just in case."

He went to take the saddle out of Georgie's hands, but she refused.

"I'm going to be Dominic Blackwell's groom this week," she said. "So I might as well get used to doing all the work."

"So this Blackwell guy, he's, like, a top showjumper?"

"Uh-huh," Georgie said. "I'll be working for him for six weeks and if he gives me a good grade then I'm through into the second-year eventing class – otherwise, well, I'm just through."

"So you're working for him during school?"

"Uh-huh," Georgie said. "And after school and weekends – you know, helping out at the competitions."

"So I should expect to see you again when? Next Christmas, maybe?" Riley said sarcastically.

"It won't be that bad!" Georgie was taken aback. "We'll figure something out."

Riley looked doubtful. "I hardly get any time with you, Georgie. All the other guys at my school are always taking their girls out on dates. We never go anywhere together."

"We're together now," Georgie said. "I bet most

girls don't get up at four a.m. to be with their boyfriends!"

Riley looked hurt. "I thought you liked coming to Keeneland Park."

"I do!" Georgie groaned. "And I don't need to go on a date with you. I'm happy just being here like this. It's not my fault that I have school and this apprenticeship – this is who I am, Riley."

"I get that," Riley said. "I guess I was hoping you'd be able to help me out over the next few weeks with Marco's training."

"I'll try," Georgie said, "but this apprenticeship is really important."

"So the Firecracker isn't important?" Riley frowned. "It's a $232,000 race. I think it's a bit more important than impressing some showjumping guy."

Georgie felt herself getting flustered. She took a deep breath. "Listen, can we not get into a fight about this?"

Riley didn't say anything. He cast a surly glance at his watch. "It's almost six thirty. I'll mix Marco's feed and then we'll go."

The drive back to Blainford was tense and silent. But

eventually, as they got closer to the school, Riley's mood seemed to thaw a little.

"So, anyway," Riley said, as he pulled up outside Badminton House to let her out. "I could really do with someone for Marco to race against. I was thinking that maybe you could come out again with me and ride Talisman?"

"When?" Georgie asked.

"Monday? Pick you up after dinner? We can give them an evening workout under the lights."

Georgie was going to be crazy busy on Monday. It was their first day of the apprenticeships and she had Belle to look after and schoolwork too, but after the conversation she'd just had, she didn't really see how she could say no to Riley.

"OK," she smiled and kissed Riley goodbye. "See you then."

✳

At midday on Monday Alice and Georgie were waiting in front of the red Georgian brick buildings of the Academy for the minibus to take them to their apprenticeships.

"I can't believe I've got stuck with dressage," Alice groaned.

"I can't believe I got stuck with Kennedy," Georgie said as she watched the showjumperettes approaching.

Georgie noticed that Kennedy Kirkwood had somehow managed to substitute a pair of expensive navy Animo breeches with Swarovski crystals on the pockets for her regulation jods. She wore her glossy red hair loose and flowing over her shoulders as well – not very practical when she was about to spend the afternoon mucking out Dominic Blackwell's stables.

As the minibus pulled up in front of the school buildings, Kennedy tried to push her way past Georgie and Alice.

"What's the hurry, Kennedy?" Alice said. "There's no first-class section on a minibus. You'll have to sit in economy with the rest of us."

There was a titter from the crowd of eventers waiting to get onboard. Kennedy shot the girls a filthy look.

"Tell your sidekick to watch her mouth or she'll end up on Fatigues with you," Kennedy told Georgie.

"You can't give Fatigues. You're not a prefect, Kennedy," Georgie glared at her.

"Her boyfriend is!" Arden, ever the lapdog, leapt to Kennedy's defence.

Kennedy stepped past Georgie to take up position at the front of the queue. "Just because Tara has stuck us together doesn't mean I have to be nice to you," she sniped.

"Trust me," Georgie said, "that never occurred to me."

Kennedy and Arden took their seats at the back and Georgie stopped by the driver's seat to talk to Kenny.

"I hear my nephew's got that little chestnut lined up for the Firecracker," Kenny said. Or at least that was what Georgie thought he said. Kenny had a mouthful of chewing tobacco and it was hard to understand him at the best of times.

"Uh-huh. I went along to Keeneland Park to watch Riley breeze him yesterday," Georgie said, "He's pretty confident that Marco can win it."

"Here's hopin'," Kenny said. "Clemency Farm sure could do with some good fortune right now."

Georgie was going to ask Kenny what he meant by that, but there was a queue of riders behind her waiting to get onboard so she moved on.

Kenny set off down the driveway, steering the minibus along the broad tree-lined driveway of the Academy out the front gates and back towards the main road heading for Versailles. The distinctive dark-stained post and rail fences of the Academy gave way to the white post and rail fences of the surrounding bluegrass horse farms. This district was the best breeding pasture in the world for young Thoroughbreds. Over five hundred horse farms jigsawed in side-by-side into this tiny district.

Although the stables were state-of-the-art, from the outside these bluegrass farms had an honest, old-fashioned look about them with clusters of white wooden barns and red rooftops dominating the fields.

With so many top flight farms so close together it didn't take long for Kenny to do the rounds, dropping off the students at their appointed employers. He had dropped off half of his passengers by the time he reached the farm gates of the Blackwell Estate.

Two white Doric pillars topped with the giant golden initials D and B marked out the front gates, and instead of a limestone driveway like most farms in the district, the path to the stables and the house was tarmac. As the minibus eased up the drive Georgie saw black and silver stable blocks, a tennis court and a swimming pool, and a house that looked like a giant iced wedding cake, with more massive white columns running along the front.

"Georgie and Kennedy?" Kenny drawled, "This one's your stop."

Georgie grabbed her bag and followed Kennedy off the bus.

The doors eased shut the minute that they got off and Kenny was gone, leaving the two girls alone in front of the wedding cake's front door.

"Nice house," Georgie said.

Kennedy gave a hollow laugh. "You're kidding me! A tarmac driveway? That's so tacky! Totally nouveau riche. I mean, who decorated this place? Simon Cowell?"

Georgie had never thought about the social

implications of tarmac before, and she was still boggling over this when Dominic Blackwell appeared from the stables.

"My new grooms have arrived!" he said, extending a hand to shake. "Julie and Kelly, yes?"

"Georgie and Kennedy," Georgie smiled.

"Close enough," Dominic Blackwell said, clearly not too pleased about being corrected. "Follow me, girls. You're about to enter the best stables in the Northern Hemisphere!"

From the outside, the stables looked like a modern art gallery – or maybe a top secret aircraft hangar – all jet-black aerodynamics and cool steel. Dominic Blackwell pressed a button and the sleek sliding doors eased back.

"I've got nine horses in work," he told the girls. "The feeding schedule must be kept precisely. All loose boxes and equipment must be maintained to a meticulous standard. Blackwell runs a tight ship!"

Georgie looked around the stalls. The horses were gorgeous and the place was immaculate.

"How many other grooms work here?"

"Normally I have three or four grooms," Dominic

Blackwell hesitated, "but at the moment, Blackwell is having a few… staffing issues."

"Oh," Georgie said. "So how many other grooms are there right now?"

"As of this moment?" Dominic Blackwell raised both hands and pointed at Georgie and Kennedy. "Two."

"Just us?" Georgie squeaked. "Looking after all of this?"

"Right! Follow me…" Dominic Blackwell ignored her comment and began to stride through the stables, giving a whirlwind tour. "The haylage is kept in the outdoor barn. The horses are boxed 24/7 and require four feeds a day. All feed formulations are written up on the whiteboard in the tack room. All tack must be polished before being put away. Hooves must be oiled and Stockholm tarred each night. Manes must be pulled and kept no longer than ten centimetres or a handspan wide and tails bobbed at the hocks. I like my horses plaited for events and I always require quartermarkers with my initials on their rumps…"

The list of duties and the exacting way in which Dominic Blackwell wanted the tasks around the yard executed seemed to be endless and incredibly complicated. Georgie grabbed the notebook and pen out of her backpack and scribbled as fast as she could, taking copious notes on Dominic Blackwell's likes and dislikes, and the various requirements of his nine horses.

Kennedy, meanwhile, wandered along like she was being given a tour of a particularly dull museum, barely looking at the exhibits as she strolled through. She was ignoring everything that Dominic was telling them; a fact that hadn't escaped him. When she gave a theatrical yawn as he was explaining the routine for mucking out the boxes, he finally called her on it.

"I'm sorry, Kelly," Dominic glared at her, "but if my little tour is boring you, perhaps you'd like to return to the Academy and we can finish this apprenticeship right now before it's even started?"

Kennedy gazed back at her new boss with supreme confidence.

"My name isn't Kelly," she said. "It's Kennedy – Kennedy Kirkwood. I believe you know my stepmother, Patricia Kirkwood?"

Suddenly, Dominic Blackwell's whole demeanour changed. His frown disappeared and was replaced by a charming smile.

"Patricia Kirkwood's stepdaughter!" he said gaily. "Well, imagine that! And how is darling Patricia these days?"

"Very well, thank you," Kennedy replied. "She's been sponsoring Hans Schockelmann the showjumper for a long time now, as you probably know. She just bought a new horse for him to ride. His name is Tantalus. He's worth..."

"$15 million," Dominic Blackwell finished her sentence. "Hans Schockelmann is one of my great rivals on the circuit of course. Blackwell would love to be given the ride on Tantalus. Do let your stepmother know that Blackwell has the best stables in the Northern Hemisphere and Blackwell is available should she ever want to change her sponsorship at any stage in the future."

"Thank you, Dominic," Kennedy said. "That's so sweet of you! As you might have guessed I do hold a lot of influence with my stepmother. She's really excited about this apprenticeship and is very keen that I do well on my placement."

"Well, I'm sure your stepmother won't be disappointed," Dominic Blackwell said, "...in fact, she'll be thrilled when you tell her that I have appointed you to the role of head girl."

Head girl.

Georgie couldn't believe what she was hearing. In a professional stables the head girl was a very important and senior position above all the other grooms. The head girl was an experienced horsewoman who knew everything about workout routines, stabling, feeding regimes, and the general business of running a yard. Making Kennedy the head girl on the first day like this was a joke!

"Julie," Blackwell said turning momentarily to Georgie. "Grab a pitchfork and start clearing the dung out of the boxes."

He turned back to Kennedy. "Let me introduce you to the horses, Kennedy, and then you can help me with the afternoon workouts while Julie does the feeds."

"My name is Georgie," Georgie muttered. But Blackwell didn't hear her. He was too busy introducing his horses to the new head girl.

Chapter Five

Alice Dupree sat in the minibus with a sense of impending doom. Ever since she had been assigned to apprentice to dressage rider Allegra Hickman she'd decided there was just one reasonable conclusion to be reached.

Tara Kelly must hate her.

What other explanation could there possibly be for lumbering Alice with the very worst assignment in the whole class?

If dressage was a vegetable, it would be Brussels sprouts. It was like torture – Alice had Caspian sitting idly in the stables when they should be doing cross-country lessons and here she was stuck with dressage grooming for a whole term!

With a thundercloud hovering over her head, Alice got off the minibus at Allegra Hickman's front gates. She was in such a foul mood that it took her a while to notice how nice the place was. There was a little white cottage with a wraparound veranda at the front, and a driveway edged by a hedge smothered in tiny white flowers led to the barn and stables out the back. The stables were big enough for eight horses and there was a concrete wash-down bay and a space to park the horse truck. It was all very basic, except for the dressage arena which was Olympic-sized.

In the arena, astride the most enormous black horse Alice had ever seen, was Allegra Hickman. She was wearing white jodhpurs, an old faded yellow shirt and a baseball cap on her head instead of a helmet. She sat in her dressage saddle with her legs long and straight, her hands held up delicately in front of her, as if she were proffering a silver cocktail tray filled with drinks. She had the most amazing posture, her spine erect and her eyes dead ahead as she came down the long side of the arena in a lovely extended trot and then headed towards a long bank of enormous mirrors that lined the far end of the arena. Once the black horse was positioned in front of the mirrors, Allegra Hickman slowed him down and began to trot on the spot, looking at herself in the mirror to check her position and the movement of the horse. The black horse lifted his white-bandaged legs in a perfect piaffe, then Allegra urged him seamlessly into a canter and began to weave sideways across the arena in a balletic half-pass.

As they reached the long side of the arena, Allegra spotted Alice standing and watching them. She pulled the black horse to a halt and then relaxed the reins so the horse could stretch his neck as she walked over to join her new apprentice.

"Hi!" she said. "I'm almost done. There's a seat over there."

Alice looked over beyond the flowering hedge and saw a cute white wooden shed that looked a bit like a bus stop – a dinky shelter with a wooden bench seat at the side of the arena. She made her way over and sat down on the bench to watch Allegra finish the workout.

Allegra picked up her reins and the black horse elevated into the air like a hovercraft and floated across the school. The dressage trainer drove forward with her legs and held the black horse with her hands so that the energy collected beneath her. The great black stallion was like a coiled spring as they moved their way across the centre of the arena in a series of perfect one-tempi changes.

"I'm trying to get him to use his hindquarters more," Allegra called out to Alice as she rode the flying changes. "Sometimes he has a tendency to be a little downhill and I really have to work him to keep him in front of my legs."

Alice nodded but she had no idea what Allegra meant. As far as she could tell the horse looked perfect.

Allegra cantered around the arena and came down again to try the tempi changes once more. The black horse flung out his front legs like a schoolgirl doing double-dutch over a skipping rope.

"That was much better!" Allegra seemed pleased. "Did you notice how nicely he lifted his knees?"

As she continued to school the horse Allegra kept her focus but managed to also keep talking simultaneously the whole time to Alice. Even though it all looked perfect from the sidelines, Allegra was hyper-critical of her performance and was constantly pointing out when the horse performed nicely and when his movements needed improvement. "That pirouette was a bit rushed – my fault!" she would say. Or "watch how his trot improves when I ask for more energy…"

Alice found it surprisingly interesting to watch with Allegra's running commentary.

"This horse, Virtuoso, has just started competing at Grand Prix level so he knows the movements but he needs to establish them and make them second nature," Allegra told Alice as she pushed the black stallion sideways in a canter half-pass all the way to the centre line and then back again in the opposite direction.

"Now that was a perfect half-pass, good lad!" She pulled the horse up to a walk and gave him a slappy pat on the neck to reward him. "Very good, Virtuoso!"

Allegra came over to the bench seat and dismounted.

"Right!" she said. "Your turn!"

"Me?" Alice squeaked. "I'm only grooming for you."

"Not at this yard," Allerga countered. "One of the perks of being on my team is that you get a regular private lesson. So why don't you mount up and we'll get started."

"Ummm," Alice wasn't sure how to phrase it without being rude, "I'm not really that into dressage."

Allegra arched a sceptical eyebrow. "No, of course. You're an eventer, aren't you? Don't worry – I know the score. I was a Blainford pupil myself years ago and I don't imagine things have changed. The eventing kids all think they're far too cool to do anything except jumping – leave the dressage to the geeks, huh?"

"Umm, yeah, kind of." Alice admitted.

Allegra shook her head in disbelief. "Well then, little miss eventer, why don't you get onboard and show me what you've got?"

She held out the reins and Alice ducked through the white post and rails fence and stepped on to the soft sand surface of the dressage arena.

"I'll leg you up," Allegra offered.

Alice was about to say that she didn't need it but then she noticed the size of the black horse. Standing next to Virtuoso was like standing beside a mountain.

"I know, he's big," Allegra said, clocking Alice's

expression. "Seventeen hands. A typical warmblood in both build and temperament too. He's quite... opinionated."

In the saddle, Alice's legs didn't even reach the stirrup irons. Allegra had to shorten the leathers by four holes.

"You'll learn to stretch and ride with your legs in the longer position while you're here," Allegra told her, "But for now you can keep your stirrups short."

Settling into the saddle, Alice picked up the reins and asked Virtuoso to move forwards. As soon as she put her legs on he stepped violently sideways underneath her.

"Too much with the right leg," Allegra corrected her. "He thinks you want him to do a pirouette. You must be careful, Alice, he's so finely tuned that if you move your legs or your hands in any direction, or so much as lighten your seat bones to one side then Virtuoso will take that as a cue. Now, put your legs on lightly together and ask him to move forward at a walk and then go into trot."

Alice tried again. She wrapped her lower legs around the enormous girth of the black horse and with the gentlest squeeze she asked him to walk and then asked again to trot.

The power of the horse beneath her felt like a rocket igniting its thrusters. Virtuoso's strides almost took her breath away as he sprang forward into a trot that was so elevated and graceful the horse seemed to almost float in the air between strides. Alice had to gather her wits about her to stay with him as he flew along the long side of the arena.

"That's good," Allegra said. "Don't try to slow him down. I know his movement feels huge but you must keep your legs strong. Ride him from the hocks! Balance him back with your seat! Now bring him across the arena and ask him to extend that trot."

Alice turned across from the corner of the arena and clucked with her tongue. "Come on, boy!"

Baffled by her aids, Virtuoso suddenly tried to launch into a canter, and then, when Alice panicked and pulled back on the reins, he threw his head up in the air.

Alice kept a firm grip and tried to regain control with the reins, but now Virtuoso really took offence. As his rider flailed wildly to control him, Virtuoso mistook her confused cues as a request for a pirouette and in a swift, single manoeuvre the massive black horse began to pivot on his hindquarters and fling his front legs around so that he was spinning in a circle. Alice lost both her stirrups and suddenly fell forward on to his neck.

Virtuoso gave a startled snort and then launched himself straight up into the air with a massive buck. Alice had nothing to hold her in the saddle and went flying through the air. Her last thought before she hit the sand was that it was a very long way to fall off this big black horse.

One thing eventers know how to do though is fall off. Alice landed with a tumble roll and was on her feet again before Allegra Hickman had reached her side.

"I'm OK," Alice said, dusting herself off, feeling slightly shaken. "I just wasn't really expecting that."

"Neither was he!" Allegra Hickman replied. "If you bounce around on his back like that then you're going to be eating sand every day for the rest of term."

Alice looked hurt. "He's a difficult horse."

"He's not," Allegra Hickman disagreed. "But if you

make a mistake he'll call you on it straight away just like he did today. Don't be afraid of that – you can use it to your advantage. If you ride him well, he'll reward you for it."

"He looked so easy when you were on him," Alice realised how lame this sounded as soon as the words left her mouth.

"That's the whole point of dressage," Allegra Hickman replied. "You do it well and make it look easy, when in fact it's the hardest thing in the world."

Allegra put a firm hand on Alice's shoulder. "Ready to get back up there?"

Alice looked nervous. Allegra smiled. "I'm gonna uncover your inner dressage geek, Alice Dupree – just you wait and see."

Dominic Blackwell currently had four Grand Prix mounts: Maximillion, Polaris, Cameo and Cardinal, and five other extremely valuable up-and-coming Warmbloods in his stable.

"Nothing but the best, that's Blackwell's motto!"

Blackwell told Georgie. "Blackwell has an eye for quality horse flesh."

More like an eye for other people's chequebooks, Georgie thought.

She knew that in the real world most professional riders didn't own their mounts. But it was the way that Dominic Blackwell talked about his horses as if they were money in the bank – just possessions instead of personalities. He spent his whole day on the phone making ingratiating cooing noises to appease his rich sponsors and hardly paid a blind bit of notice to the actual horses themselves.

Blackwell was in this sport for the money and prestige and it was clear that the lure of Patricia Kirkwood was driving him crazy. He literally fell over himself treating Kennedy like a princess, immediately giving her the riding duties on his second-string horses.

Georgie tried not to dwell on the unfairness of this as she mucked out the stables like Cinderella with a pitchfork in her hands. It wasn't that she minded the hard work, but when the final scores were tallied at the end of term there was no doubt which one of them would be getting the better mark from Dominic Blackwell.

Tacking up the gorgeous horses in the stables so that Kennedy could ride them almost broke Georgie's heart. She would have loved the chance to get onboard any of the exquisite showjumpers in Blackwell's string.

Kennedy, of course, was entirely unimpressed by the opportunity she'd been given. One horse was the same as the next as far as she was concerned.

It's not that Kennedy's a bad rider, Georgie thought. It was more that she lacked a natural empathy for the horses that she rode. She'd been given lessons by some of the best instructors in the world but Kennedy still tended to ride robotically and treat every single horse as if it were exactly the same as the last. Compared to a rider like Riley, Kennedy had no instinct or feel.

Not that Dominic Blackwell seemed to notice. He had the same loveless attitude to horses as Kennedy. Meanwhile Georgie was back on the ground in the stables, shovelling dung and filling haynets.

You shall go to the ball, Cinders, she told herself as she filled yet another barrow with manure that afternoon.

But that seemed as unlikely as a mouse turning into a coachman. How was she going to win Dominic Blackwell over when all she ever did was clean out his loose boxes? She was at the bottom of the apprentice heap right now and unlucky Georgie looked doomed to lose.

Chapter Six

"Are you coming to dinner or not?" Alice asked impatiently as she held the bedroom door.

"I don't think I can move," Georgie groaned, lying face down on the bed.

Her body ached from the afternoon spent shovelling dung and polishing tack, but it was more than that.

Alice rolled her eyes. "Listen, my apprenticeship sucks too, you know."

"I thought you said Allegra was cool to work for?" Georgie said, not moving.

"She is," Alice said. "But it's still dressage. I'd much rather be on a showjumping yard."

"Not on Blackwell's," Georgie groaned. "I can't believe he made Kennedy his head girl!"

"Yeah, yeah, it's a travesty," Alice said dryly, "now pull yourself together, we're leaving."

Georgie groaned and dragged herself up.

Daisy and Emily joined them on the front steps of the boarding house and the four girls made their way up the driveway towards the dining hall.

An endless stream of complaints punctuated their walk from Badminton House to the main school grounds as the girls compared aches and pains.

"You should see the inside of my thighs!" Emily said. "They're virtually purple with bruises. Tina Dixon is obsessed with doing sitting trot with no stirrups. I spent half the afternoon trying to stay onboard this bonkers mare of hers while she kept telling me that all I needed to do was relax and stop gripping with my thighs."

"At least your injuries are from riding," Georgie said. "I broke my back trying to muck out the loose boxes while Kennedy got to ride all afternoon."

"Georgie, don't let her take advantage!" Emily insisted. "Tell Dominic Blackwell that it's not fair and you should both be doing stuff equally."

"It's no good," Georgie groaned. "Dominic knows

who her stepmum is and he's being totally greasy. Kennedy has convinced him that she's his access-point to endless riches and that she can get him the ride on Tantalus. He's so busy sucking up to her he can't even be bothered with me."

"You just need to impress him," Alice said.

"How? With my dung-shovelling abilities? He can't even get my name right!"

"Well, what are you going to do?" Emily asked.

"Georgie's just gonna have to cope. Georgie has no choice. Georgie needs to suck it up," Georgie replied.

"Why are you talking like that?" Emily frowned.

"That's how Dominic talks!" Georgie giggled. "He refers to himself in the third person!"

Alice pulled a face. "You're not serious?"

Georgie began to imitate him. "Blackwell has the best stables in the Northern Hemisphere! Blackwell runs a tight ship! Blackwell is... a total nutter as far as I can tell. Honestly, I am so knackered. I'm going straight to bed after we do our homework."

"Ohmygod!" Emily suddenly remembered, wincing. "Sorry Georgie, I forgot to tell you. Conrad was looking for you earlier on. He said to tell you that you're supposed to report to the Burghley House tack room tonight to do your fatigues."

Georgie had survived a day of hard labour, slogging while Kennedy rode. And now her rival's vindictive prefect boyfriend was going to make it worse. Her misery was complete.

Georgie concentrated on stabbing her pasta with her fork and glumly followed the conversation over dinner that evening. Daisy proved to be a welcome distraction as she was telling the Badminton House girls about her first day with polo rider Seb Upton-Baker.

"He wanders around the yard in these tight white breeches like someone out of a Jilly Cooper novel," Daisy said rolling her eyes. "All the girl grooms follow him around like dogs with their tongues hanging out. I think they only work there in the hope that he'll ask them out."

"Including you?" Alice asked.

Daisy looked insulted. "Eww! He's, like, twice my age!"

"You could do worse than a jet-set international

playboy," Alice laughed. "His last girlfriend was a supermodel."

"I'd rather be a polo player than go out with one," Daisy replied sniffily.

"You are a polo player," Emily pointed out to her. "We're in the school team, remember?"

"A proper player, I mean." Daisy said. "Seb is an eight-goal player and the way he rides is totally amazing. I tried to play stick and ball with him and some of the other grooms. I thought I would know the ropes from the Bluegrass Cup but this high-goal stuff is so much more intense. And you should see the way he runs the stables. The grooms treat those ponies like gold."

"Well, I fell off a seventeen hand horse today," Alice said. She seemed remarkably cheery about it. "Allegra let me ride Virtuoso. He's her Grand Prix horse. He can do the most incredible stuff like flying one-time changes."

Emily grinned, "I thought you found dressage boring?"

"I do. I mean I'm not into just trotting around like a

dullard, but the way Allegra explains all the fancy moves is kinda interesting," Alice admitted.

"What bothers me about this whole apprentice thing is when do we get to spend time with our own horses?" Georgie said. "I won't get the chance to ride Belladonna this term if I'm spending all my time in lessons or at Blackwell's yards."

"I know!" Emily agreed, "Barclay is hardly getting any work and he goes a bit bonkers after too many days without riding."

"We should get up early and ride before school," Alice suggested.

Georgie hadn't thought of that. "Are we allowed?"

"We're not allowed out on the cross-country courses," Alice said, "but surely we can use the indoor arena?"

"Good plan," Daisy agreed.

"And let's set up some jumps!" Alice grinned. "I'm desperate to jump something!"

On the way back down the driveway the girls discussed the details of their morning ride. At the point where the driveway branched off towards the Burghley House stables Georgie peeled off from the group.

"I better go straight to the stables and face the music," she sighed. "I'll catch you guys—"

"Hey!" Emily interrupted, "Isn't that Riley's pick-up?"

Georgie looked down the driveway. There was Riley's red truck parked outside Badminton House.

"Ohmygod." Georgie suddenly had an awful sinking feeling. "I completely forgot! I told Riley I would ride trackwork with him tonight."

As she walked towards the boarding house Georgie saw Riley climb out of the driver's seat and give her a wave. She waved back, her heart racing, palms sweating. Somehow she knew this wasn't going to go well.

"What do you mean you can't come?" Riley's face fell. "You said you wanted to help me to train Marco…"

"I know," Georgie said, "but I've been so busy I just forgot and—"

"You forgot!" Riley's expression was incredulous. "I tell you that this race is crucial and it just slips your mind that you're supposed to help me train for it?" He raked a hand through his hair in exasperation. "Geez, Georgie!"

On the gravel outside Badminton House the other three girls stood about looking uncomfortable.

"You know what," Emily said, "we'll see you later, Georgie."

"Yeah," Alice agreed. "Come on, Daisy."

Daisy seemed to be enjoying her ringside view of the confrontation and looked disappointed at being forced to leave. "OK," she sighed, "but it was just getting good!"

The girls went up the front steps leaving Riley and Georgie alone. The silence was deafening. Finally, Georgie spoke.

"I don't know what else I can do, Riley," Georgie sighed. "I said I was sorry. I'm saying it again. I'm really sorry, OK?"

"Fine," Riley said. "Just put your jodhpurs on and we'll go now. We can still make it to Keeneland Park in time to get a couple of laps of the track in."

Georgie shook her head. "I can't, Riley. I've got Fatigues."

Riley's face fell even further. "Who gave you Fatigues?"

"Conrad."

Riley was furious. "Is he still giving you a hard time? Georgie, why didn't you tell me?"

"Because I knew you'd be like this!" Georgie said. "He's a prefect, Riley, and… you don't understand."

"Why?" Riley said. "Because I don't go to Blainford?"

"Yes!" Georgie said. "Riley, this is my world. I'll deal with Conrad."

"So this is your way of dealing with it? By letting me down?" Riley said. "Well done, Georgie. You've clearly got everything under control. I'll back off and get out of your way!"

He walked around to the driver's door of the pick-up.

"Where are you going?" Georgie couldn't believe he was storming off.

"I'm going to the track to ride my horse," Riley said.

He held the car door open for a moment and then said. "You know what, Georgie? I think we're both under a lot of pressure. Maybe we need a little break."

"I know," Georgie agreed, "but I can't take time off until the end of the term and…"

"No, Georgie," Riley said softly, "I meant a break from each other."

Georgie's eyes went wide. "Oh." She felt herself

trembling all of a sudden. "Are you… are you breaking up with me?"

Riley shook his head. "No… maybe… I just think we need some time apart."

"Do I have a choice?" Georgie asked.

Riley hesitated at the door of the pick-up and Georgie wished he would stop and turn around, but he didn't. "I'll see you later, OK, Georgie?" he said with sorrow in his voice. "You take care."

And before Georgie could say anything more, he'd started the engine and driven away.

Walking back up the driveway towards the Burghley House stables Georgie was shaking, fighting back the tears. Riley had just split up with her! Or had he? He said he wanted to take a break – what did that mean? A break was just a cowardly way of saying that he didn't want to be with her any more. She felt numb with shock. This couldn't be happening.

Georgie walked through the stables and headed for the tack room. There was no sign of anyone and when she reached out a hand to try the door it was securely locked.

"Oh this is just great!" Georgie shook the door furiously. She could have gone to the track with Riley after all!

She was storming back through the stables to leave when she ran head first into Conrad Miller.

"Going somewhere, Parker?" Conrad's tone was supercilious.

"I didn't think anyone was turning up," Georgie said.

"Well, I'm here now," Conrad said. "Follow me."

He walked through the stables and unlocked the door to the tack room, holding it open so that Georgie could follow him inside.

The Burghley House tack room was a long, narrow space with saddle racks lining the walls.

"You're on saddle-cleaning duty," Conrad said, lifting a saddle down off the rack and propping it on the floor in front of Georgie. "You'll find the kit in the box by the door."

Georgie groaned. "Why am I cleaning a Burghley House saddle?"

"Because," Conrad said, "Prefects don't have to clean their own saddles. That's what first years are for…"

As he said this, he lifted down another two saddles off the top racks.

"You can do these two as well when you finish that one."

"I'll be here all night!" Georgie was horrified.

"There were supposed to be two others on Fatigues but they got excused," Conrad said. "So I guess that means you've got their work to do too."

By the time Georgie had soaped the saddles and had stripped the stirrup leathers off and begun to oil them with the lanolin cream her arms were aching and her hands were cramping.

Conrad, meanwhile, was comfily sat on top of a pile of saddle blankets stacked on an old tea chest in the corner of the room. Sitting cross-legged, his long black boots folded underneath him, he flicked his way through a book, making notes as he went on a lined pad on his knee.

"What are you reading?" Georgie asked.

Conrad looked up at her and scowled. Even when

he wasn't angry, Conrad had what could only be described as fierce features – a hawk-like nose and strong brow, offset by a square jaw-line that managed to rescue his other features by putting them into proportion at least. His russet hair was an odd colour, neither brown nor red – if he was a horse then Georgie would have said he was a liver chestnut. To say he was good looking would be pushing it, but he was... strangely attractive, Georgie supposed, in a weird Conrad-ish way.

"What are you reading?" Georgie tried again and Conrad held up the cover of the book so that she could see it. It was the famous German dressage rider Reiner Klimke's best-selling book: *Cavaletti – schooling horses over ground poles.*

"I've got that book," Georgie said. "It's good."

Conrad's scowl deepened. "You haven't studied this yet. This is a senior text," he said.

"I have a copy of my own that my mum gave me," Georgie said. "I like the chapter about different ways of using cavaletti stacked on a circle."

Conrad's scowl eased. "Have you tried riding the jumping exercises?"

"Not yet," Georgie admitted.

"We've been doing them in class with Bettina Schmidt," Conrad said, looking genuinely excited. "Bettina's really into Reiner Klimke. She's got the video that goes with the book – it's brilliant."

"I've seen him ride," Georgie said. "Well not in real life obviously, but there's some great old footage of him competing at the Olympics when he was young – he was pretty cool."

"His daughter is an eventer," Conrad said, "She rode at Badminton last year..."

For the next hour as she cleaned tack, Georgie found herself doing something she never thought possible – enjoying a conversation with Conrad. There was something so touching in the way he talked about his riding, and especially his new horse, a big grey called Sauron.

"Sauron is really sensitive," Conrad said. "He bucked me off twice this week – but it wasn't his fault..."

Conrad spoke about Sauron the same way that Georgie did about Belle and suddenly she realised that he had a genuine love for his horse.

They had been talking about horses for almost an hour when Conrad shifted the subject to Riley.

"Are you still going out with that guy?" he asked Georgie. "You know, the one with the attitude problem?"

"His name is Riley," Georgie said. And then, letting her guard down, she added, "and, no, I don't think I am. I think we just split up."

"You think?" Conrad pulled a face. "Don't you know?"

Georgie sighed. "He kind of split up with me. Just before, in fact, when I was on my way here."

"Well... he's an idiot," Conrad said. And then he added. "A girl like you is way out of his league. If he had half a brain he'd realise that."

As they'd talked, Conrad had been watching Georgie struggling to reattach a pair of stirrup leathers to the stiff bars of the saddle.

""Let me give you a hand with those," he said.

"No, it's OK. I've got it..." Georgie tried to force the leathers back but her hands were so cramped and sore she could barely move her fingers. The leathers were stiff, despite the saddle soaping and she couldn't get them through.

"Here, let me help," Conrad put his book down and came over to help her.

"No, honestly, I can do it," Georgie insisted, gripping the saddle and trying to force the leather. Conrad reached down to take the saddle out of her hands and Georgie pulled it back towards her again.

"Why do you have to be so stubborn all the time?" Conrad said, still hanging on.

"And why are you always trying to push me around?" Georgie wasn't letting go.

She was standing there, face-to-face with Conrad, defiant, looking him in the eye. He leaned closer and took a firm grip on the saddle, his hands clasping over her own. "Come on, Georgie, stop being silly."

It was the way he said her name. Not Parker. *Georgie*. She released the saddle and as she let go, she expected Conrad to back away but he didn't. Instead he moved closer and closer. And then, before she knew what was happening, Conrad kissed her.

Maybe it was the shock of feeling his lips against hers,

but for the briefest moment, Georgie kissed him back. And then, in a rush of awareness, she gasped and reeled backwards.

"What did you do that for?" She looked at Conrad, wide-eyed.

"I just thought…" Conrad looked puzzled. "You know there's always been something between us, Georgie."

"The only thing between us was that saddle," Georgie's heart was racing, "and it should have stayed between us! Ohmygod! That should never have happened!"

Conrad smiled. "You're cute when you're angry," he said.

"Well, you should know," Georgie shot back, "you're the one who makes me angry."

"Exactly!" Conrad was still smiling. "We have a love-hate relationship."

"No, Conrad," Georgie said, "We have a hate-hate relationship."

"Same thing."

Georgie was beside herself. "Conrad, I have a boyfriend!"

"You *had* a boyfriend," Conrad corrected her.

"Whatever!" Georgie snapped. "You have a girlfriend!"

Conrad shrugged. "Kennedy'll get over it. She's only dating me because I'm a prefect."

Georgie looked at him with astonishment. He couldn't be serious! Conrad? And her? There was no way.

"I've gotta go." Flustered and feeling slightly hysterical, Georgie snatched up her school cardigan and pulled it on as she headed for the door.

"Wait, Georgie," Conrad was smirking. He was acting like it was all a massive joke. "You can't go. You've got Fatigues, remember?"

But Georgie kept going. She was out the door and gone, her heart pounding as she ran through the stable block and outside into the fresh air.

For the past three terms, ever since she got to Blainford, Conrad had gone out of his way to try to make her life hell – and now, in his own way he had finally succeeded.

Chapter Seven

Alice was horrified.

"Georgie! What were you thinking?"

"I didn't have a chance to think!" Georgie said. "One minute Conrad's helping me with the stirrup leathers and the next minute he's suctioned on to my face!"

They were saddling up the horses for their early morning riding session, and in between putting on her martingale and adjusting her tendon boots Georgie had told Alice everything.

"What am I going to do?" Georgie groaned.

"Do you want to date Conrad?" Alice asked, but immediately knew the answer from the look on Georgie's face. "OK, OK, just checking."

"How am I going to tell Riley?" Georgie groaned. "He's already hardly speaking to me!"

"Tell him you were cleaning a saddle and you tripped and fell and Conrad's lips got in the way?"

"Very funny."

"Well tell him nothing then! He'd just broken up with you. It's none of his business."

"I can't do that," Georgie shook her head. "The next time Conrad sees Riley he'll be bound to blab."

"They might not run into each other again," Alice said. "And besides, Conrad might not say anything."

"You really think so?"

"No, who am I kidding?" Alice shook her head. "Conrad will hold this over you – or he'll tell Riley just to pick a fight." Alice shook her head. "I don't see how you've got a choice. You'll have to tell Riley yourself."

"Can't we go with the 'don't tell him' option?" Georgie frowned. "I liked that one better."

"Georgie, I know you – you won't be able to lie to Riley. Tell him that it was a mistake. You were upset because he said you were on a break and Conrad got the wrong message."

Georgie bit her lip. "You're right. I'll tell Riley. I'll explain that it was nothing. He'll understand."

"Tell Riley what?" Emily said as she led Barclay out of his box and into the corridor.

Georgie looked mortified.

"What are you guys talking about?" Emily persisted.

"Is something going on?" It was Daisy, joining the group.

"Last night in the tack room," Alice said in a hushed voice, "Georgie kissed Conrad."

"Eww!" Emily shrieked.

"I didn't!" Georgie protested. "He kissed me!"

"Oh yeah," Daisy said sarcastically, "when you put it that way it sounds much better."

"Listen," Georgie said. "I know it's gross. It was one of those weird things that – look I'm not going to go into details – it was a mistake, OK? I just want to get back with Riley and put it behind me so please, please don't tell anyone."

Emily looked genuinely relieved. "So you're not dating Conrad?"

"No!" Georgie groaned.

As Georgie rode Belle into the arena she felt so good being up on her horse once more. There was no better place to clear your head and forget all your problems.

After working their horses around the arena at a trot to loosen them up, they began schooling the horses back and forth across the low jumps they had constructed.

Belle was still only a six-year-old, but already her jumping genes were plain to see.

This was gymnastic training, which meant keeping the fences low, but even so Georgie was impressed by the athleticism of the mare beneath her. If she asked Belle for an extra stride the mare would oblige and stretch out. If she sat back and held her steady, Belle would shorten up again instantly.

The communication between the girl and the mare was so subtle that if you had watched them together popping over the coloured rails you wouldn't have noticed the quiet conversations between them. Their dialogue was no longer the tense argument it had once been. It was soft and private, and all Georgie needed was a touch of her hands to check the mare, or a tap of the heels to send her forward. At the end of their hour-long jumping session Belle hadn't refused a single fence or done more than scrape a rail. And Georgie had forgotten all about Riley and Conrad and the kiss.

Georgie felt acutely aware of Kennedy's eyes on her as she climbed onboard the minibus that afternoon. She walked down the aisle of the minibus but when she reached Kennedy's seat the showjumperette put an arm across to stop her.

"Hey Parker!"

Ohmygod she knows!

"Did you enjoy your fatigues?"

Kennedy looked smug as she said this and Georgie realised that she had no idea what had happened in the tack room yesterday.

"Let me through, Kennedy."

Kennedy shook her head. "You have to say please. Otherwise I'll get my boyfriend to put you on Fatigues again."

Georgie felt the guilt welling in her stomach. "Trust me, that's the last thing anyone wants."

Kennedy narrowed her gaze. "What do you mean by that?"

In the aisle behind Georgie the last rider finally boarded the minibus and Kenny put his foot down. The bus gave a sudden lurch forward and Georgie gratefully sidestepped Kennedy and her questioning and took a seat.

Horse dung is a metaphor for my life, Georgie thought ruefully as she rolled up her shirtsleeves at Blackwell's yard and set to work forking lumps of poo into the wheelbarrow.

Yesterday Georgie had been furious that Dominic Blackwell had unfairly given the job of head girl to Kennedy. Today, she felt so bad about kissing Kennedy's boyfriend that mucking out the stalls felt like what she deserved.

Like most horsey girls Georgie found the warm grassy aroma of horse dung faintly appealing. But at Dominic Blackwell's place the stench overpowered her. She seemed to spend her afternoons knee-deep in it, digging her way out while Princess Kennedy did no yard work at all.

The final straw that afternoon came just after Georgie had finished the marathon task of mucking out and refreshing the nine boxes and sweeping out the central corridor. She finally had everything done when Kennedy swept in on her horse alongside Blackwell chatting and laughing and when Blackwell dismounted and flung his reins mindlessly at Georgie, Kennedy imitated him and did the same thing!

"Hey!" Georgie was stunned. "I'm not your groom, Kennedy."

"Not yet," Kennedy said. "But if you play your cards right, maybe I'll give you a job when you leave school."

And at that moment, Georgie stopped feeling guilty. She was wasting time worrying about hurting Kennedy Kirkwood's feelings – Kennedy didn't have any. Hadn't Conrad admitted that Kennedy was only dating him because he was a prefect?

It was time to pull herself together. Kennedy may have taken the first round of the apprentice – but this battle was far from over. Georgie was ready to make a comeback.

For the past week at Allegra Hickman's yard, Alice Dupree had noticed a change in her riding. Alice came from a long line of showjumpers and eventers – and she felt most comfortable in a jumping saddle with her knees tucked up high into the roll pads, her seat tilted forward in two-point position.

Alice owned a dressage saddle but she'd never really liked riding in it. She hated the way the saddle's long, lean flaps and deep-bucket seat seemed to lock her into place on the horse.

"You have a forward seat," Allegra Hickman had told her on that first day when she rode Virtuoso. "Showjumping has ruined your position – but I can fix it again."

Allegra walked over and grabbed Alice's leg by the ankle.

"Your foot," she said, "should be *here*, not here." She shoved the ankle back and twisted it. "And the knee needs to open off the saddle and relax. That's it! Better!"

Allegra put her hands on Alice's hips. "Now imagine

your hips are a bucket and there is water inside them. Which way is your water tipping?"

Alice thought about this. "Forward."

"Well, straighten up!" Allegra said. "Keep the water in your imaginary bucket. Sit perfectly upright. Now take hold of this."

Allegra passed Alice a slim wooden stick. "Tuck it behind your back. That's right!"

Alice threaded the slim bit of wood so that it passed behind her back beneath her shoulder blades and was held secure in the crooks of her elbow when her hands held the reins.

"You'll ride with this bit of wood until your back is no longer bent like a banana," Allegra told her. "It's going to hurt at first, but you'll get used to it."

This was a phrase that Alice heard a lot of that week. Allegra said the same thing when she made Alice ride without stirrups. Or when she made her ride with one hand tucked behind her back, or her knees held out off the sides of the saddle or, worst of all, wearing weighted Dyna-bands that made her muscles stretch and strain.

As far as Alice could tell, the pain never got any less. But by Friday she realised that her posture was erect, that her back was ramrod straight, her seat was deep and her legs were long.

"Now," Allegra said, "you're beginning to look like a dressage rider and the real work can begin."

The routine at the Hickman yards had become second nature to Alice. She would arrive and set to work straight away, doing a quick muck-out of the loose boxes before tacking whichever horse Allegra had chosen for her to ride.

Allegra spent an hour each day giving Alice a dressage lesson. It was a luxury for any apprentice to have so much time devoted to them and Alice knew it.

"I learned to ride dressage under the great Magda van der Camp," Allegra told Alice. "Everything I know, I learned from her. It's our role as riders to pass on our knowledge to the next generation."

After her lesson with Allegra was over, Alice would have a lengthy list of stable chores to get through. She would tack up all of the horses that were listed on the stable whiteboard for Allegra to ride that day. There were usually two or three of these in the afternoon schooling session and Allegra would work each horse for about an hour. Once Allegra was finished, Alice untacked each horse and scrubbed the concrete stable block floors, polished the tack and did the grooming and rugging up for the night. Then Allegra would have a brief chat about the day with Alice before Kenny arrived to pick her up in the minibus.

By the end of Friday, despite the mammoth workload, Alice had an extra spring in her step. Her lesson that day on Virtuoso had been better than just good – it had been amazing. She had ridden a flying change in the arena – something she had done many times on showjumpers, changing their canter lead to prepare for a jump, but never quite like this before. With Allegra barking orders at her about placing her legs one way and then the other she had cantered the big, black stallion across the arena and he'd flung his front legs out in mid-stride, swapping legs so seamlessly that, as Allegra said, "if you were riding in a real Grand Prix test you would have just earned yourself a nine for that movement!"

She had been so fired up by her ride that Alice whipped through her chores in record time. Allegra was schooling her advanced-level mounts today, and Alice wanted to watch her ride Esprit, a stunning but volcanic liver chestnut gelding.

Alice rugged the last of the horses and then walked briskly through the stable block and along the pathways until she reached the little shelter with the wooden seat and plopped down to watch.

Allegra trotted Esprit around the arena, on a loose rein at first allowing the big liver chestnut to stretch his neck low and deep and round. Alice watched with fervent admiration as the great trainer began to collect the liver chestnut up, driving him harder with the legs and shortening the frame of the great horse. He looked so lovely with his tail swishing from side to side as she rode, the rhythm of his strides as regular as a metronome, his knees lifting up in a beautiful exaggerated trot.

And then, suddenly, the tail began to swish a bit more than it ought. It was a sign that the horse was under pressure, that he was unhappy.

Alice cast her eyes to the front end of the horse and noticed that something very strange was going on. Allegra Hickman had been riding Esprit so that his neck arched beautifully, but now the horse's outline had changed. Allegra was being hard with her hands and forcing the horse to arch his neck in an unnatural way, stretching it so much that his chin almost touched his chest. The horse was curled up as tight as a seashell and his tail was swishing back and forth as he tried to show his discomfort. But Allegra didn't seem to notice – or if she did, she was choosing to ignore the horse's complaints. She kept his head screwed down in the severe arched position and then began to twist it, keeping it tucked to his chest but now making the horse canter with the head bent hard to the inside on one rein and then hard to the outside on the other.

Watching the display, Alice felt more and more unsettled. Allegra couldn't keep riding poor Esprit like this. Every muscle in the horse's neck and back must be aching by now.

But Allegra didn't stop. She kept the horse overbent at the poll so that his chin was almost tucked up against the poor creature's forelegs. After another fifteen minutes of being ridden like this Esprit seemed to be barely able to breathe. He was choking with a hideous froth on his lips, his eyes glazed and ears flat back as he submitted to the cruel hands that held his head.

Alice knew what she was witnessing. It was a riding method that had once been famed for getting amazing results in the dressage ring – but the controversial technique was considered so inhumane and cruel that it had been banned in competitions throughout the world after a public outcry. Never in Alice's worst dreams did she think she would see it being ridden in real life. Certainly not by the woman who, until a moment ago, she had respected and trusted. But she couldn't deny what she saw before her. Allegra Hickman was using rollkur.

Chapter Eight

The Badminton House girls were at their usual dinner table when Alice joined them. She flung down her tray and threw herself into the seat next to Georgie.

"What's up with you?" Daisy asked.

"Nothing," Alice said unconvincingly. She picked up her cutlery and then changed her mind and put it down again.

"What do you guys think about rollkur?" she asked suddenly.

"I think it's gross!" Daisy said.

"It's been banned, hasn't it?" Georgie asked.

Emily looked puzzled. "What are you talking about? What's rollkur?"

"I mean it's illegal, right?" Georgie asked.

"Totally," Daisy agreed.

"Uh-uh," Alice shook her head. "The FEI banned riders from doing it at competitions in the warm-up arena, but there are no regulations about riders doing it at home."

"Hello?" Emily was losing patience now, "Are any of you going to tell me what you're on about? Is rollkur a piece of riding equipment? A breakfast pastry?"

"It's a style of dressage riding," Georgie said, "where the rider forces the horse's head into an unnaturally low position so that they overbend their necks and tuck their chin all the way down to the bottom of their chest."

Emily winced. "Why would you do that? It must hurt them!"

"Some of the most famous dressage competition riders in the world do it," Alice said. "They claim it doesn't hurt if you do it right. I mean, they would never hurt their best horses on purpose."

"Yeah, right!" Daisy scoffed. "I've seen pictures of horses being ridden in rollkur and it looked like torture to me."

Georgie nodded, "You'd have to be a total monster to do it."

Emily looked across the table at Alice who seemed to be growing more and more upset. "Why did you want to talk about rollkur, anyway?" she asked.

Alice was about to speak, and then she changed her mind. She stood up and picked up her tray.

"Alice?" Emily frowned, "What are you doing? You only just got here!"

"I... I'm not hungry," Alice said. "I'll see you guys back at the boarding house. I've gotta go."

Georgie had tried so many times to call Riley, but he was never home – or he wasn't answering his phone. He never returned any of Georgie's messages.

"Give him time," Alice insisted without realising the irony. This was Riley's biggest complaint – that Georgie didn't share her time with him. Although she had to admit that he had a point. Her days were full from the moment she woke up and headed to the stables to ride Belle in their early morning jump-schooling sessions.

Then she had morning classes at school and the afternoons spent doing hard labour at Blackwell's yards until Kenny picked them up in the minibus again and got them back to Blainford just in time for dinner. After that, there was just enough time to fit in a gruelling two hours worth of homework before collapsing into bed. When exactly was there time for a boyfriend?

Georgie was exhausted. She had just finished two hours of maths and English homework and was in her pyjamas about to get into bed when she heard the tap on the window. It sounded like a pebble against the glass. When a second pebble struck, Georgie walked over to her bedroom window and saw Riley standing on the lawn.

"Hey Georgie!" Riley smiled up at her as she pushed the window open.

"What are you doing here?" she hissed. "You'll get me kicked out of school!"

"You'd better let me in then," Riley said, "before someone sees me."

Georgie looked around her messy bedroom. Her towel

was hanging off the end of her bed and she grabbed it and poked one end out the window.

"Hang on to this and climb up," she told Riley. The window was only a metre and a half off the ground outside and Riley had no trouble scaling up the wall and scrambling inside.

"This is fun," he said as he straightened himself up and took a look around. "Like Romeo and Juliet."

"I'm pretty sure I don't remember Juliet using a bath towel in the version we studied," Georgie said. It seemed strange having a boy in her room. Even stranger when that boy was Riley and the last time she'd seen him he'd driven off in a huff.

"I've wanted to talk to you all week," Riley said, "but I've been working late at the stables every night and there's a nine o'clock cut-off for the phones here so I couldn't get through. Tonight I was driving home and I couldn't stand it any longer. I figured I'd just swing on by and tell you my news…"

Riley cast his eyes around the room and his expression changed suddenly when he saw the poster above Georgie's dressing table.

"You have a Justin Bieber poster in your room?"

Georgie panicked. "It's not mine. It's Alice's."

Riley seemed to accept this excuse and grinned. "Guess what? Marco qualified! We're through. We're going to be racing in the Firecracker!"

"Ohmygod!" Georgie leapt across the room and hugged him hard. "Riley that's so cool! I'm so happy for you."

Riley hugged her back. "I'm really sorry for freaking out at you like that the other day, Georgie. I know I said some awful stuff I didn't mean. I'm just under so much pressure at the moment."

"I know," Georgie said, "I understand."

"No, you don't," Riley let her go and she saw now just how serious his expression was. "The Rainmaker totally whipped Marco in the Hanley Stakes and we're up against him at the Firecracker. In the Hanley, we were in the lead all the way in the home straight and then that black horse seemed to come out of nowhere. He beat Marco by three lengths – it was like we were standing still. We have to find a way to beat him."

"Does your dad have any ideas?" Georgie asked.

"Dad's got enough on his plate," Riley said. "There's all this stuff that's been happening at the farm. The bills have really been stacking up lately. It's not cheap running racehorses and the books haven't exactly been balancing for a while. My dad's too proud to say anything to me but I know he's been selling off horses to cover the debt. That's why this race matters so much to me. If Marco and I could win the Firecracker then I could put the money into the farm with dad – maybe even become his business partner."

Riley met her gaze. "I've got a lot riding on this, Georgie, and I need you."

It had always been Georgie that needed Riley – it had never occurred to her that he might need her too.

"The race is a month away," Riley said, "Saturday the 23rd at three in the afternoon. You can come to it, can't you? You're my good luck charm."

"Totally," Georgie's cheeks were flushed with excitement. "I wouldn't miss it for the world!"

Riley looked really pleased. "I'll get you tickets. You

can sit with my mom and dad in the owners' stands," he told her. "And bring Alice and Daisy and Emily too if you—"

"Shhh!" Georgie held up her hand to silence him. There was the sound of footsteps right outside.

"Ohmygod. The housemistress!" Georgie hissed. "I am in so much trouble if she finds you in here."

In a panic, Riley flung himself across the room and hid behind the door, as the handle turned and it swung open.

"Oh thank god it's you!" Georgie said as Alice walked in.

Alice looked confused. "Who else would it be?"

"I thought it might be the house mistress," Georgie said. Then she reached out and swung the door shut and Alice leapt back in shock.

"Riley! What are you doing in here?"

"I came to see to Georgie," Riley said. "We had some stuff to talk about."

"Oh!" Alice suddenly looked anxious. "Oh, well… that's great… because talking is good. That's what I said to Georgie. I told her that she should tell you."

Riley was confused. "You did?"

Georgie shook her head. "No, Alice. I don't think this is what you think it is..."

But Alice was babbling. "I mean it was all Conrad's fault – and anyway it didn't mean anything. It was just a stupid kiss."

Riley's eyes widened. He turned on Georgie. "You kissed Conrad?"

Alice realised too late what she had done. "Ah... sorry! I thought you said you'd talked!"

Riley's face was stony. "So when exactly were you going to tell me about Conrad, Georgie? When you dumped me for him?!"

"No!" Georgie was horrified. "Conrad was just a mistake. You and I had had that stupid fight and you told me you wanted a break and I had Fatigues and it... it just happened."

"I tell you I want some time out and half an hour later you're making out with that creep?"

"Not making out! It was one pathetic kiss and it wasn't my fault!"

Georgie was beside herself. "This is why I didn't tell

you because I knew you would think it meant something more. It doesn't matter."

"You don't get to decide what matters to me, Georgie!" Riley shouted.

"Hey, umm, guys, if we could just keep our voices down?" Alice suggested. "Getting kicked out of school for having a boy in our room is not really part of the plan."

"Don't worry about that," Riley said, stomping across the room. "I'm leaving."

Georgie's eyes welled with tears. "Riley, I'm sorry."

Riley turned back to face her. "You know, Georgie, maybe we should take a break."

Georgie was stunned. "A break? You're splitting up with me? Again?"

"I mean it this time, Georgie."

She could feel the tears coming now. "Riley, no…"

And then there were more footsteps outside the bedroom and a knock at the door.

When Mrs Birdwell the house mistress entered the room just a few seconds later she found the two girls alone in their bedroom, Georgie with a tear-stained face, and the curtains fluttering over their open window. Riley was gone.

The atmosphere was bleak at Dominic Blackwell's stables. Blackwell's cold-hearted approach to his horses continued to appal Georgie. He never gave them as much as a pat on the neck at the end of an intensive training session.

When Georgie remarked on this to Kennedy she just shrugged. "He's a professional," she said. "What do you expect?"

"My mum was a professional rider and she still loved her horses," Georgie had offered in reply. Kennedy had rolled her eyes at this. "Well it's a shame you can't go and work for your mom, isn't it?" she sneered.

As a result Georgie found herself being extra snuggly and attentive to the horses in Blackwell's stables. She was starting to get to know them by now, and each of the horses had their own quirks. Cameo, the bay Hanoverian Grand Prix mare was her favourite. She had a sweet, even nature and would close her eyes and doze blissfully as Georgie groomed her around her bridle path and down her white blaze. Polaris was a gentle giant, a seventeen-two hand chestnut that whinnied as if he was starving whenever Georgie dished out his hard feed and nickered gratefully as he shoved his nose into the feed bucket.

The only horse in the stables that Georgie didn't like handling was Maxi. The big grey Holsteiner could be bullish and unpredictable. Twice now Georgie had to fling herself to the far side of his loose box to get out of the way of a sudden strike from his front hooves.

Georgie was doing exactly what every good groom should do, getting to know each of the horses in her care, understanding their individual needs and what made them tick. But none of it seemed to impress her boss. By the end of the first week, Blackwell was solely focused on wangling an invitation from Kennedy to join the Kirkwood's next summer holidays in the Bahamas. As for Georgie, he gave her about as much attention as he gave his horses and she was almost resigned to changing her name to Julie.

"No, no make him halt, Alice!" Allegra Hickman shook her head in disbelief. "What on earth is wrong with you today?"

Alice had arrived at Allegra's yard that afternoon feeling confused. She was in awe of Allegra's skill as a Grand Prix dressage rider, and yet she felt conflicted. Georgie and Daisy had both been adamant that rollkur was wrong but should she trust her friends or the woman who was fast becoming her mentor?

"You are so tense up there your whole position in the saddle is falling apart," Allegra said, striding over to take Virtuoso's reins. "Something is clearly bothering you, so why don't you tell me what's wrong?"

"There's nothing bothering me," Alice replied feebly.

"Alice," Allegra shook her head, "your words are telling me one thing but your body is telling me another."

Alice looked extremely uncomfortable. "I don't know how to say this…"

"Cut to the chase, Alice," Allegra was losing patience.

Alice took a deep breath. "OK, I saw you riding… on

Friday... you were in the arena schooling Esprit and you were... ummm..."

Allegra frowned, "I was what? Come on, Alice, spit it out!"

"You were doing rollkur!"

"Oh. I see," Allegra said. "And I take it that you're opposed to rollkur, is that right?"

Alice didn't know what to say. "I guess."

"The way that I ride is challenging for those who do not understand, Alice," Allegra said, "but I had hoped that you would be smart enough to grasp my methods."

Alice's heart was racing. "I know you're a great rider, Allegra, but the way the horse was bent over like that seemed really unnatural..."

"What is natural?" Allegra asked. "Think about human athletes, and the way they train. If you are a runner you don't just run, do you? You lift weights to build muscle and do stretches to get limber."

Allegra paused. "My horse is an athlete and rollkur helps to train every muscle in his body. Yes, the techniques might possibly be dangerous in the wrong hands but I'm not some rank amateur!"

Allegra Hickman looked disappointed with her pupil. "Alice, where are these accusations coming from? You've seen me ride. My horses look happy, don't they?"

"Um, I suppose so," Alice said. She wanted to mention the swishing tails and the flat-back ears that she had seen on that Friday afternoon but maybe she had exaggerated these things in her mind. After all, this was the great Allegra Hickman that she was talking to – one of the best dressage riders in the world. Alice was beginning to feel very silly and more than a little ashamed for bringing it up.

"I didn't mean to upset you."

Allegra Hickman shook her head. "Please don't apologise. I'm glad that you asked me about this, Alice. I want you to understand the importance of hyperflexion. Once you are ready, you will be able to use it too and then you will see what a great suppling and submission aid it can be to create the perfect dressage horse."

She looked up at the girl still sitting on the big black horse. "Trust me, Alice," she reassured her. "I am one of the best dressage riders in the world. I think I know what I'm doing, don't you?"

Alice nodded.

"Good!" Allegra looked pleased. "Dismount and let's untack him. I have some caramel cookies waiting for us in the kitchen. What do you say, my star apprentice?"

Alice gave a half-hearted smile. "Thank you."

Chapter Nine

Georgie had been thinking about her disastrous visit from Riley and she'd come to the conclusion that their break-up was all her fault.

"No. It's my fault!" Alice insisted as they walked to the stables together. Alice had already apologised a million times for sticking her foot in it and telling Riley about Conrad. But Georgie had insisted that Alice didn't have anything to be sorry about.

"I needed to tell him and I just didn't know how," Georgie said. "At least now he knows."

"But you didn't mean for this to happen," Alice said. "Conrad's the one with the 'busy lips' and you're paying the price."

Georgie wished more than anything that she could

erase the kiss with Conrad – but in a strange way one good thing had come out of the incident in the tack room that day. The conversation that she'd had with the Burghley house prefect had jogged Georgie's memory about her Reiner Klimke book, and when the girls started their early morning showjumping sessions she had pulled out her old copy and found the chapter on gymnastic cavaletti for showjumpers. The book showed step-by-step pictures on how to set up cavaletti to encourage the horses to be elastic and lengthen or shorten their stride on command and use their backs and necks properly over fences.

The Klimke book quickly became their bible for the morning workouts and soon the girls could see the results. Their horses were rounder and softer when they jumped and Georgie was constantly amazed at just what a clever athlete Belle was proving to be. The mare always put her feet in the right place to get herself out of trouble and never refused a fence.

"If only Dominic could see the way I've been jumping on Belle, he might give me the ride on one of his horses," Georgie told Alice.

Friday marked the end of the second week of their apprenticeships and at Blackwell's yard that afternoon Georgie celebrated this anniversary by tidying the tack room. She had spent hours cleaning it from top to bottom when Dominic Blackwell stuck his head in.

"Ah, Julie," he said. "Make sure you loop the reins *through* the nosebands before you hang the bridles up, please. It all looks very sloppy the way it is now. And store the numnahs in a separate stack from the other saddle blankets. It's much neater that way." He shook his head. "It could really do with a clean-up in here, Julie."

"Yes, Dominic," Georgie replied as sweetly as she could through her gritted teeth. Just the other day he had told her specifically not to separate the saddle blankets and numnahs. It was classic Dominic Blackwell. He always changed his mind and acted as if he'd said the same thing all along – there was no use arguing with him.

"Oh, and Julie?" Dominic added, "Can you come down to the arena once you're done. I'm going to brief you and Kennedy on the game plan for tomorrow."

Tomorrow? But that was Saturday. Georgie hastily re-stacked the blankets and tidied the bridles and then headed down to the arena where Dominic was riding one of his young mid-grade horses, a grey mare called Flair, while Kennedy was working a handsome dark chocolate brown appaloosa with a lovely white blanket on his rump around the arena over the jumps. The appaloosa's name was Star Spangled Banner – Banner for short.

"I'm taking the mid-grade horses to a qualifier tomorrow at the Kentucky Horse Park," Dominic said. "So I will need both of you onboard as grooms. You'll need to be here by six am. Julie, I want you to pack the truck tonight. We'll need all the usual kit."

"Kennedy," he turned to her, "as head girl you're in charge. Team Blackwell must run like clockwork. I'm relying on you. Don't let me down."

Georgie had never been to the Kentucky Horse Park before and she was dying to check it out. In the heart of bluegrass country, the Horse Park had been the venue for the 2010 World Equestrian Games and was the home of the famed Kentucky Three-day Event.

As they drove in through the competitor's entrance, Georgie could see the four-star cross-country course in the distance, and ahead to the right, the stables which housed hundreds of horses during the big events at the grounds. She could also see the massive indoor stadium that accommodated thousands of spectators who came here to watch everything from Western cutting horses to gymnastic teams performing dramatic acrobatics on the broad backs of vaulting horses.

The most popular dates on the calendar at the Horse Park were the days of the Grand Prix showjumping series when all the seats would be sold-out to a maximum capacity crowd.

Today's showjumping was a mid-grade qualifier, but there was still a reasonable turn-out in the grandstands, with a couple of thousand spectators gathered to watch the day's competition.

"Do you think your stepmum would like tickets to watch me ride here in Kentucky the next time she visits you?" Dominic asked Kennedy as he drove the horse truck through the gates. He'd been working his way up to this for weeks and now he was really putting the pressure on for Kennedy to introduce him to Mrs Kirkwood. But the more he pushed, the more disinterested Kennedy became.

"She's pretty busy with Hans Schockelmann," Kennedy said. "So I hardly ever see her. She never comes here. She spends most of her time in Paris these days."

Dominic Blackwell was taken aback. "Well," he said tersely. "Why don't you ask her and we'll see?"

"Yeah, whatever," Kennedy said casually.

Dominic Blackwell scowled. He'd put a lot of effort into being nice to this girl to get closer to the Kirkwood fortune but it didn't appear to be paying off. He was beginning to think he'd been wasting his charm on this feckless red-headed child. "There's our parking space," said Georgie, pointing out their allocated spot beside the day pens. Dominic parked the truck and set off for the registration tent, leaving the two girls to unload the horses.

Blackwell had brought along his second-stringers and up-and-comers, the horses that needed experience and points on the scoreboard in order to rise up the ranks.

There were four horses on the truck and two of them Georgie knew already. Star Spangled Banner, the mare that Kennedy had been riding the other day, was an Appaloosa Warmblood. Flair was a Selle Francaise. Both of these horses were on the cusp of progressing to the big league and today Dominic Blackwell would be jumping them over fences set at a metre thirty.

The other two horses were more of an unknown quantity. Navajo, the big bay mare with the wide, white blaze, was well-bred but relatively unproven. The Optimist, a novice chestnut gelding, was a horse that Dominic Blackwell had taken on behalf of a sponsor. From the way he talked about the chestnut it was clear that he didn't think much of the horse's abilities.

Georgie led Star Spangled Banner and Flair down the ramp and tied them side-by-side along the right hand wall of the truck.

She could see Kennedy dithering about with the other two horses.

"Tie them up next to these two," Georgie instructed.

Kennedy did this, but then stood about looking lost and useless. Georgie soon figured that Kennedy had probably never groomed at a competition before – Kirkwoods were used to employing grooms, not being grooms themselves.

Georgie, on the other hand, had grown up attending competitions with her mum. Ginny Parker had proper professional grooms helping her, but she'd always given her 'little junior groom' jobs to do like filling the horse's water buckets or sorting out sets of tendon boots as a way of keeping young Georgie occupied during long days at events.

Georgie hadn't realised at the time, but watching and helping the professional grooms at work had been an education. From the moment they arrived at the Kentucky Horse Park, Georgie instinctively knew the drill. She immediately got to work grooming the horses and marking the DB chequerboard pattern on to their glossy rumps before wrenching studs into the bottom of the horses' hind shoes for better grip when they were jumping. As she worked away, Kennedy stood by looking gormless.

"Kennedy," Georgie finally lost her cool. "Stop standing around and do something!"

Kennedy looked genuinely baffled. "Like what?"

Georgie tossed a tub of tiny black rubber bands to her. "Take these and go and plait Banner's mane!"

Reluctantly, Kennedy picked up the tub and headed to the other end of the truck to start plaiting up Banner.

Georgie, meanwhile, plaited up the other three horses, moving along the line doing tiny braids and then rolling them up and securing them with the bands into tight and precise plaits – an odd number along the neck plus one for the forelock. By the time she had finished she found Kennedy still only halfway through Banner's mane.

"Kennedy!" Georgie couldn't help it. "What's taken you so long? I've already plaited three horses!"

"She won't stand still," Kennedy complained. "She keeps fidgeting. She's going to stand on my feet!"

Georgie sighed. "You go and start unpacking the tack then, and I'll finish plaiting her."

Kennedy wasn't happy with this solution. "You can't give me orders, you know," she said, "I'm the head girl, not you. You go and do the tack! I'm going to finish plaiting."

As she was carrying the saddles out of the truck, Georgie had glanced over at Kennedy and thought there was something weird about the way that she was plaiting Banner's mane. The plaits were a bit of a mess and falling apart – but it was more than that.

Kennedy had finished the whole neck and was doing the forelock when Dominic Blackwell returned. He took one look at Banner's plaits and totally exploded.

"What have you done, Kennedy?" Blackwell roared. "You complete moron! You've plaited the mane on the wrong side of the neck!"

Kennedy had failed to notice that Star Spangled Banner's mane had fallen to the left side by mistake and she had braided in the plaits to the left. The horse's mane should have been swept over to the right side. And by the way Dominic Blackwell went on, you would have sworn life and death were hanging in the balance!

"Undo the plaits and start again!" he fumed. "I'm not riding into that arena with a mane like that."

Dominic Blackwell took a closer look at Kennedy's

atrocious plaits, the bits of hair poking out and the rubber bands coming undone and he revised his orders. "Get Julie to redo them – she's better at plaiting than you are. You can bandage the legs."

Kennedy had no choice but to step aside and Georgie took over, re-plaiting the entire mane on the correct side.

Meanwhile, having been reassigned to leg bandaging, Kennedy made a complete hash of that too. This time Dominic took one look at the wobbly bandages that were gappy and twisted with bits hanging out and made Georgie step in and unwrap and do them again.

Kennedy spent the rest of the morning in a sulk doing the only job that Blackwell trusted her with, pre-mixing the hard feeds and filling the hay nets and buckets of water. And even then Blackwell asked Georgie to keep an eye on her.

Georgie worked like a dog that day, constantly covering up Kennedy's mistakes. But it was when the competition got underway that her skills really came into play. Georgie knew the ropes from the years working with her mum and she remembered what Ginny Parker always used to say: that a great groom didn't need to be asked for anything because they were always one step ahead of their rider.

Georgie was exactly that, anticipating Dominic Blackwell's needs and accurately delivering what he wanted. The minute that Blackwell emerged from the arena after a showjumping round she would be there to take the reins of his horse and hand him a bottle of water. She had the horses all tacked up and ready to go the moment that he needed them.

Blackwell never said thank you – but Georgie could tell that he was pleased with her even if he wasn't prepared to show it.

Kennedy, however, was not so lucky. She had been worse than useless all day, but there was an aura about her, as if she assumed that her family connections made her immune to Blackwell's vicious attacks. She was about to discover just how wrong she was.

It was just before the one metre thirty class for novice horses and Dominic had instructed Kennedy to wait for him at the gates with Flair so that he could swiftly switch horses once he'd completed his first round on Banner.

As the applause signalled the end of Dominic's clear

round he came cantering out and did a leaping dismount, throwing the appaloosa's reins at Kennedy. Then he grabbed Flair's reins from her, stuck his foot in the stirrup and bounced up on to the back of the grey mare.

He was about to go into the arena when suddenly he wheeled Flair around to face Kennedy.

"This horse has no martingale!" he said.

Kennedy was taken aback. "But you don't ride Flair in a martingale. I've never seen you use one on her at home."

"You brainless girl," Dominic Blackwell snapped. "I don't ride her in a martingale at home, but I always use one when I'm out competing."

"But you didn't tell me to put one on her!" Kennedy frowned.

"And I'm supposed to tell you everything, am I?" Blackwell said. "I suppose I should tell you to put a saddle and bridle on too, should I?"

Kennedy should have just apologised, but she was a Kirkwood and it wasn't in her family's nature to know when to shut up. "If you want a martingale on your horse then you need to tell me," she insisted.

"Stop arguing and get out of my sight!" Dominic

Blackwell dismissed her with a wave of his hand. "Take the appaloosa back to the truck and send Georgie over with a martingale now!"

Georgie hadn't seen any of the drama at the ringside, and when Kennedy arrived at the horse truck she was bent down re-wrapping Navajo's bandages.

"Hey!" Kennedy stomped over to her. "Why didn't you tell me that Flair needed a martingale?"

Georgie stood up. "She does? Blackwell's never ridden her in one before."

"Yeah well, Dominic's having a wig-out over at the arena," Kennedy snarled. "He wants you to take one to him straight away."

Dominic Blackwell's face was a mask of rage by the time she arrived. "Forget it!" Blackwell snarled at her. "I'm due in the arena now! I don't have time to dismount so you can put it on."

"It's OK," Georgie began hastily strapping the martingale around Flair's neck. "I know a way of putting it on fast – just stay in the saddle."

As Georgie flitted about fastening buckles and straps to get the martingale intact Blackwell looked genuinely impressed. The martingale was attached in less than a minute and Blackwell's name was now being called for the last time, requesting his presence in the arena.

"Good work, Julie," he said as he headed in through the arena gates. "Now go and get my next horse warmed up for me."

"What?" Georgie couldn't believe it. Blackwell's next horse was Navajo. "But Dominic, that's Kennedy's ride – I've never been on Navajo!" Georgie hadn't been on any of Blackwell's horses. He'd never even allowed her to hack out a horse at the yards and suddenly she was his warm-up groom?

"You heard me!" Blackwell snapped. "I want you to ride her. I don't have time to discuss this!"

And with that, Dominic Blackwell rode into the arena on Flair and left Georgie on the sidelines, gaping like a stunned mullet.

She headed back to the truck, where she found Kennedy tacking up.

"What did he say?" Kennedy asked.

"He wants me to ride Navajo," Georgie said.

Kennedy looked genuinely shocked. "You? But that's ridiculous. You've never even been on her before!"

"I know," Georgie agreed. "I tried to tell him that – but you know what he's like."

Kennedy narrowed her eyes. "You did this on purpose! You're trying to make me look bad!"

Georgie shook her head, "Kennedy, honestly I'm not! I'm not the one doing this – it's Dominic's idea!"

"Oh, whatever!" Kennedy thrust the reins at Georgie. "Take her then! And don't expect me to help you!"

As she led Navajo over to the practice arena Georgie felt her stomach knotting with nerves. She had to get on this unknown mare in the tense environment of the warm-up arena and get her going nicely. Now that she had been given the chance to impress Dominic Blackwell she didn't want to blow it.

Georgie stuck her foot into the stirrup and bounced up on to the mare's back. Navajo was sixteen-two hands high and solidly built and it felt a little bit like sitting on a mountain. The mare's neck seemed to stretch out ahead of Georgie forever, and the barrel of her ribcage and belly felt broad between her legs. Georgie adjusted her stirrups, tightened the girth and then moved the mare on into a walk and then a trot. Her strides felt massive and it took a moment for Georgie to find her centre of balance.

Looking out for the other riders, Georgie found a clear space and started to work the mare around in a circle at the trot, but it was impossible to do a full circle without the other competitors cutting in on her space and getting in her way.

"Sorry!" Georgie pulled Navajo up to a sudden stop to let another rider past. The rider on a big grey glared back at her.

"Oops!" she winced as yet another rider on a black horse cut right in front of her this time, riding at a canter, leaving Georgie with no choice but to abruptly change direction to avoid a collision.

Trying to find a quieter space, Georgie tried moving around to different corners of the arena until finally she recognised the truth. There was nowhere to go. The whole warm-up arena was a nightmare. Riders kept hogging her space and no one seemed to care about being polite! They were all fighting for every scrap of arena that they could find, and Georgie was being pushed around. She needed to harden up if she was going to stand a chance of getting her warm-up done.

Pushing Navajo into a trot, Georgie put her mental blinkers on and traced out a circle on the mare, riding her in a twenty-metre loop on the sand. She kept circling and this time, when other riders ducked or weaved in front of her she just kept going and ignored them. *Let them get out of the way!*

"Hey!" one woman growled at her as they almost had a head-to-head collision. But Georgie didn't even acknowledge her. She stayed in the bubble of her own world, pressing Navajo into a canter and eyeing up the practice jumps. The mare was ready to pop over a fence and Georgie was starting to get a feel for her. It was always strange to be on a new horse for the first time, figuring out their quirks and kinks. Navajo was a surprisingly sluggish mare to ride and Georgie remembered now that Dominic always rode her in spurs.

Without them, Georgie had to really push the mare into her transitions from walk to trot to canter. Over the jumps though, Navajo was a wonderfully schooled ride, with a steady, rhythmic stride and a huge bascule as she curved exquisitely over the poles. Georgie popped the mare over the practice jump, a parallel bar set at about a metre, four times back and forth and then hacked the mare at a walk to the arena.

She arrived just as Dominic Blackwell turned up at the gate to look for her.

"Julie!" he said. "How did the warm-up go?"

"She's feeling great." Georgie sounded confident and professional. "She's tracking up nicely and we've been over the practice fence a few times. She's ready."

Dominic Blackwell arched a brow. "We'll see..." he said.

Georgie dismounted and Dominic bounced up onboard.

As he entered the arena, Georgie could hardly bear to watch. She knew that if Navajo put a hoof out of line then Dominic would consider it Georgie's fault!

But Navajo didn't make any mistakes. Dominic

Blackwell rode her perfectly and when they left the arena with a clear round he had a smile on his face as he waved to the crowd.

"She went very nicely indeed," he said as he pulled up alongside Georgie.

He tossed the reins to her as he walked away. "Get the next one for me and warm him up," he said. "I need to go and chat to Navajo's owner in the patron's lounge."

"But Dominic…" Georgie said. "Ummm… doesn't the head girl usually warm up the horses?"

"Exactly," Dominic said. "You're doing a good job… Georgie, isn't it? Now go and get The Optimist and take him over the practice jumps, will you? Kennedy can cool down Navajo and then polish my tack."

And with that one sentence, the tables were turned. Kennedy was no longer Dominic Blackwell's head girl. The job had just gone to Georgie.

Chapter Ten

"So you're head girl?" Alice grinned. "I wish I'd seen Kennedy's face when Blackwell told her."

"I don't know if he's told her exactly," Georgie said. "He just swapped our duties over and that was that!"

Since the mid-grade tournament Dominic Blackwell had entrusted Georgie with the schooling of his second-string showjumpers. Georgie had expected them to be a world apart from Belle, but she had quickly come to realise that anything they could do, her mare could do too. She suspected that Belle could even handle a Grand Prix level course, if she was given the chance.

The girls had been religiously working their way through all Reiner Klimke's exercises in their morning jumping sessions. They had reached the stage where they were stacking cavaletti one on top of the other to form substantial fences and were setting up complex bounce combinations in quick succession. Belle handled anything that was put in front of her with total ease and Georgie felt like the mare needed more of a challenge.

"I'd love to put the jumps right up," Georgie admitted over dinner to the Badminton girls, "and see what she can really do."

"What's the highest you've ever jumped her?" Alice asked.

"We got over the school fence that time Conrad locked us out," Georgie said, remembering that she and Belle had jumped a school gate too not so long ago, "but I think she could go even higher."

"Caspian is ready to deal with some bigger fences too," Alice agreed. "I say let's put up some real jumps and see what they've got."

"What's this? What jumps?" Alex asked as he joined the girls.

Emily looked at the other girls. "Can I let him in on it?"

Daisy sighed, "Well, you'll have to now, won't you?"

Emily turned to Alex. "You know how I've been doing jumping sessions in the indoor arena before school each morning? Well tomorrow we're going to crank the jumps up."

"Cool!" replied Alex. "Can I bring Tatou?"

"I thought you couldn't be bothered getting up early to jump with me?" Emily teased her boyfriend. "You told me that you weren't getting out of bed to go over some poxy trotting poles that a Shetland pony could tackle."

"Well, yeah," Alex admitted, "but if you're doing proper jumps you can count me in."

"What about Cameron?" Alice asked.

"He's got trackwork most mornings," Alex said. "I hardly ever see him."

"Why isn't he at dinner?" Daisy looked around. "Come to think of it, I haven't seen him in the dining hall in ages."

"That's because he doesn't eat!" Alex said as he tucked into his dinner of steak and chips. "He's been told by Frank Carsey that if he wants to be a jockey then he'll have to keep his weight down. No more chips and no more desserts." Alex forked up another mouthful. "It's not worth it if you ask me. Anyway, Cam can't come tomorrow morning."

"What's this about tomorrow morning?" Matt Garrett said as he joined the table too.

"We're having a training session with the girls in the indoor arena," Alex told him. "It's a pre-breakfast jump-off!"

"A jump-off?" Georgie protested. "Who said anything about—"

"Excellent!" Matt Garrett said. "I'm in."

"Does anyone want to explain to me how Alex and Matt Garrett have managed to hijack our schooling session?" Daisy grumbled as they tacked up their horses the next morning.

"It'll be OK," Emily reassured Daisy, clearly feeling bad about inviting her boyfriend along. "They won't take over. This is still our thing."

Emily wasn't so confident when she arrived at the

arena with the other Badminton girls and found the boys already striding out the spaces and erecting a course of jumps. They had built a short course of eight fences including a treble and a final jump that was a wide spread.

"We'll start out at a metre-twenty so that you girls stand a fighting chance," Matt said, full of bravado.

"Don't do us any favours!" Alice replied sarcastically. "Put them up to a metre thirty."

"Serious?" Matt squeaked.

"Totally," Georgie backed her up. "Let's make this a proper challenge."

As Matt and Alex went around every jump on the course raising the back poles by an extra ten centimetres the girls mounted up.

Georgie began trotting Belle around to loosen her up as the riders took turns to pop over the practice jump in the middle of the arena. Matt went first on Tigerland and jumped it cleanly.

Alex circled and followed after him. Then it was Georgie's turn. She focused on her line and rode in on a perfect forward stride. Belle jumped neatly and

Georgie asked her to come back to a halt to let the mare know that she mustn't bolt away after the fences.

"Good girl," Georgie gave her a slappy pat. They were ready.

Matt had appointed himself the first to go so the other riders sat and watched. He circled Tigerland in front of the first jump and then rode the dun gelding hard at a fast canter as if he were charging down the straight in the Grand National. A couple of strides out from the jump it became clear that Matt was coming in too fast and had judged the striding wrong. The gelding made a gallant effort but swiped the top rail down. Matt had Tigerland revved up, and he was fighting for his head and resisting Matt's hands all the way into the second fence. He took a rail down there too and Matt tried in vain to get him under control as they swept around the corner to take the third fence. Another rail fell.

By the time Tigerland was coming into the fourth fence his canter was totally bonkers and out of control, and it was all Matt could do to steer him. They virtually ploughed straight through the fence, scattering rails in their wake. Tigerland gave a deranged snort and reared up, and Matt had to throw himself forward on to his gelding's neck to stay onboard. They hadn't even finished the round and there were rails scattered everywhere.

"Cool," Alex said clapping slowly and sarcastically. "A demolition derby instead of a hunt derby."

"Hey, Matt," Alice called out, "leave some fences up for the rest of us, will you?"

Matt clearly didn't think this was funny. He vaulted off his horse and began to pick up the rails.

"A little help here?" he groaned.

"Sorry, man," Alex grinned. "You knock 'em down, you pick 'em up again. That's the rules."

As Matt rebuilt the fences, Georgie began to circle Belle, ready to take her turn. As soon as the last pole was back in its metal cup she pushed the mare into a canter and trained her eyes on the first jump.

As she came in on the approach to fence number one, Georgie felt her heart pounding. She sat up in the saddle, her legs against the mare's sides as Belle came cantering in.

"Go, Georgie!" Alice called out from the sidelines.

As Georgie turned, Belle pricked her ears and surged forward. Reacting against the sudden burst of speed, Georgie held the mare back so that Belle was almost cantering on the spot, her head high.

They were two strides out when Georgie finally let Belle go and the mare bounded forward like a gazelle, gave a grunt and flung herself into the air. They were clear and over the first fence! Belle landed on the other side. Her blood was up, and Georgie had to repeat the routine, holding her tight into the approach and only letting go at the last minute when she saw a stride. As they bore down on the third fence the mare was waving her nose in the air until right before the jump when, in a heart-stopping second, Georgie managed to get Belle back under control and over the rails.

At fence four they took three frenzied strides and Belle grazed the rails with her hind legs. The top rail dropped and the jolt was enough to spook her so that she powered forward on the other side as soon as her hooves struck the ground. The mare charged madly at the treble fence, clearing the first two elements then dropping the final rail. Georgie was nearly unseated over the penultimate jump and lost a stirrup coming into the big spread. She managed to get it back just in time and released Belle once more so that the mare flew the final jump cleanly to finish with three rails down and twelve faults.

"Way to go, Georgie!" Alice hooted.

There was a smattering of clapping and cheering from the girls and then a voice, crystal clear echoed through the indoor arena. "Well, that was total chaos!"

Georgie turned around and saw Tara Kelly. She was standing in the middle of the arena beside the other riders. She had her arms folded across her chest and she did not look pleased.

"You were barely in control for the majority of that round," Tara said. "Speeding up and slowing down all the time! What did you think you were doing letting her prance on the spot like that in front of the jumps?"

Georgie swallowed her embarrassment. "I was trying to see a stride."

Tara shook her head. "Seeing a stride is a bit like

seeing a unicorn, Georgie. You can't force one to magically appear. If you keep holding your horse like that and waiting for the moment to let go you're going to drive her mad."

Matt sniggered at this and Tara turned on him.

"I wouldn't laugh if I were you, Mr Garrett – your attempt was an even worse debacle!"

Tara looked at the assembled riders. "You've forgotten about your ribs."

Georgie frowned. She put a hand to her ribcage, prodding at them.

Tara shook her head. "Not *your* ribs. I mean R.I.B.S – as in Rhythm, Impulsion, Balance and Speed – the four keys when we are jumping."

"Oh," Georgie said, feeling a bit thick for not remembering this lesson.

Tara turned to the rest of the class. "I'm sure that Georgie isn't the only one here who needs to work on these things. So let me see all of you through the course now one at a time. And don't forget to think RIBS the whole way!"

Rhythm was at the heart of their jumping session that

morning. Tara impressed upon the class the importance of keeping the horses in a steady stride.

"Try counting your stride out loud between the jumps." Tara told Georgie as she circled Belle ready to attempt the course for a second time.

"One-two!" They took the first jump.

"Stop hanging on to her face!" Tara shouted. "Keep your legs on and stay calm in the saddle. Count your strides!"

"One-two-three-four!" And another turn to the next jump. "One-two..."

Georgie kept counting all the way to the final fence and it wasn't until she was over it that she realised how much better that round had felt.

"You had the mare going forward without a fight," Tara looked pleased. "Did you feel how much more balanced that was?"

Georgie nodded.

"Now that you actually have some control and balance we can focus on your turns. We'll make that our next session tomorrow morning."

"Tomorrow morning?" Georgie was confused.

"School regulations state that you need an instructor present at all times for showjumping in the indoor arena," Tara said. "And since you seem to be dedicated enough to get out of bed at this hour I suppose I can manage to turn up too and make this an official morning tutorial. That is, if you want it?"

"That would be brilliant," Georgie said.

"Excellent," Tara said. "Tomorrow morning at seven then."

Every morning when Georgie woke up her first thought was Riley and how much she missed him. He still wouldn't return her phone calls and if her life hadn't been such a blur of activity she would have felt totally miserable about him.

Her daily schedule was gruelling but Georgie knew it was worth it. The early morning sessions had been taken up a notch with Tara instructing. When Tara was a professional eventing rider she'd been renowned for aceing the showjumping phase, with a world-class record for always turning in a clear round on the final day.

In their second session they worked on making sharp turns.

"From the very first stride after you land you should be riding with the next jump in mind," Tara told them. "In fact, even in mid-air you should already be turning your horse where you want to go."

In just a couple of sessions Georgie's turns improved so much that she could now spin Belle on right angles straight after the jump if she needed to.

By week two Tara decided that the riders were ready for flying changes and Georgie spent lesson after lesson working to ride Belle so that she landed after a jump leading with the correct leg to tackle the next fence.

"On tight courses the ability to change legs so that you are balanced coming into a jump could be the difference between winning and losing," Tara told her class.

Georgie had been finessing her technical skills to the point where even Dominic Blackwell noticed the change in her riding when she worked his horses in the arena.

As head girl Blackwell had been assigning Georgie his best horses to ride. Of course, this didn't stop him from being vile and demanding. It was becoming clear to Georgie that Blackwell had actually been on best behaviour for those first weeks of their apprenticeship. He'd managed to suppress his worst traits then, but now they were surfacing thick and fast. He constantly contradicted himself and was arrogant to the point of being delusional. No matter how hard Georgie tried to please him he was never satisfied with her efforts. He made her clean out the loose boxes at least twice most days before he was satisfied. He would pull faces and mutter about the appalling state of the horses even though Georgie had them glossed to the level of a best-groomed trophy at any gymkhana.

Blackwell's habit of dismounting and quite literally throwing the reins at his grooms was so arrogant and awful it would have been funny – if only Georgie had someone to laugh about it with when the day was over. But all she had was Kennedy, who wasn't exactly brimming over with camaraderie. Kennedy's latest tactic seemed to be simple: do absolutely no work and drive Georgie completely barking.

"I wouldn't care if Dominic Blackwell had made you queen of England," Kennedy told Georgie when she made the perfectly reasonably request for Kennedy to tack up Maximillion. "You might be head girl, but I'm not taking orders from you."

"We're both in this together, Kennedy," Georgie had tried to tell her. "Do you want to fail the final exam?"

"If I take you down with me, it'll be worth it," Kennedy replied.

It was impossible to coax Kennedy into doing any work. Georgie suspected that Dominic Blackwell knew what was happening, but what did he care? As long as the work got done he was happy.

On a sunny Friday afternoon in the stables, Georgie was filling the hay nets when she heard the sound of footsteps behind her. She knew Dominic was still out in the arena so she assumed it must be Kennedy, skulking about. But when she turned around, she saw it wasn't Kennedy at all. Conrad was standing there, arms folded and a wry smile on his face. Georgie had the feeling he'd been standing there like that for a while.

"What are you doing here, Conrad?" Georgie felt distinctly uncomfortable being alone with him like this.

She had managed to avoid the Burghley House head prefect since *that kiss*.

"I came here to see my girl," Conrad said smiling at her.

"I'm not your…" Georgie began and then she realised what he meant.

"Oh, Kennedy," she said. "Well I don't know where she is."

"Conrad!" Kennedy called out as she skipped into view all sweetness and light. "Are you here to give me a lift back to school? Oh, thank god for that. I am so sick of riding on that smelly minibus full of morons!" She looked pointedly at Georgie.

"Come on," she pulled him by the arm. "Let's go."

But Conrad didn't move. "Wait," he said to Kennedy. "Shouldn't we give Georgie a lift back as well?"

"No!" Georgie and Kennedy both said in unison.

"Are you sure?" Conrad gave Georgie a mischievous grin. "Come on, Georgie, I'll let you ride up front with me if you want."

Kennedy pulled a face. "Are you insane, Conrad? She's said no already. Let's go!"

"Kenny will be here with the minibus soon," Georgie pointed out. "And I still have to clean out two more loose boxes."

Kennedy put her arm around Conrad and led him off down the corridor. They were almost out the door when he turned back to Georgie. Kennedy didn't see Conrad's smile as he gestured to Georgie, his hand to his face, little finger and thumb extended, smiling as he mouthed silently: "Call me!"

Chapter Eleven

*T*here were three boys' boarding houses at Blainford. Luhmuhlen and Lexington were located up beyond the fork of the driveway, but the third, Burghley House, was right beside the main school. It was a single level residence, built out of the same red brick as the school buildings and surrounded by magnolia bushes. At the front of the house there was a games room with a pool table and French doors leading out on to the lawn. Behind this room was the prefect's study and this was where Damien Danforth found Conrad Miller on Saturday afternoon.

"What do you want, Danforth?" Conrad snapped when the boy stuck his head around the door.

"There's a girl at the games room looking for you," Danforth said.

"Kennedy?" Conrad sighed. "What does she want now?"

"Not Kennedy," Damien replied. "It's Georgie Parker."

Georgie had felt totally embarrassed turning up at Burghley House and asking for Conrad. She knew that just being seen here by boys like Damien would get tongues wagging. This was James Kirkwood's boarding house – and she was desperately worried that she would run into Kennedy's brother too. But what choice did she have? She had to talk to Conrad.

At the mention of Georgie's name Conrad had smoothed a hand through his hair, checking himself out in the mirror as he rose from his chair and sauntered through to the games room.

Georgie was standing outside waiting for him. "I need to talk to you," she said.

"I thought you might," Conrad said in what he hoped was a suave James-Bondish tone. "Do you want to come in?"

"No, not here!" Georgie looked at him like he was dense. There were Burghley House second-years milling about the pool table, pretending to play as they earwigged. "Meet me in the tack room in five minutes."

"Oh right," Conrad said. "Nice and private. Good idea. I'll meet you there."

Five minutes later, Conrad arrived at the tack room to find Georgie waiting for him.

"Conrad, I wanted to…" Georgie began her sentence but suddenly she broke off, choking and gagging. "Ohmygod, what is that smell? It's like being gassed!"

Conrad looked affronted. "It's my aftershave," he said. "I thought you'd like it." He took a step closer to Georgie and she could hardly breathe. "So… you wanted to… talk?" he smiled at her.

"Yes," Georgie said briskly, taking a couple of steps backwards to get out of aftershave range. "It's about yesterday – at the stables – with Kennedy."

"I know, I know," Conrad said. "Not good."

"Exactly," Georgie grimaced. "I'm glad we're on the same page about this."

"Oh totally," Conrad said. "I mean, it was kind of funny. But it can't go on, right?"

Georgie nodded.

"I can't keep stringing her along, Georgie," Conrad said. "I'm going to have to tell her about us."

Georgie's heart suddenly stopped. "You're going to what?" she shook her head. "No, Conrad! That's not what I meant."

Conrad frowned. "You *don't* want me to tell her about us?"

"Conrad," Georgie said slowly. "There is no 'us'. There is a 'you' – and there is a 'me'. But you go out with Kennedy. There is no us."

"Oh, I get it," Conrad said. "You're not interested because I go out with Kennedy."

Georgie stared at him. This boy was as dumb as fungus. "I'm sorry, but I think that the best thing is for us to both move on. Let's not tell anyone about us, OK?"

"Gotcha," Conrad said. "I totally get it Georgie."

"So we're all good then?" Georgie said.

"Totally," Conrad said. "Trust me."

"Conrad problem eliminated!" Georgie collapsed down on her bed in the dorm rooms. "Now all I have to do is get Riley to return my calls and maybe I stand a chance of sorting this whole mess out!"

"Um... that's great, Georgie," Alice tried to be supportive, but her voice gave her away. She sounded preoccupied and miserable.

Georgie looked over at her best friend who was lying on her bed staring vacantly into space.

"Are you OK, Alice?" she asked.

"What do you mean?"

"You've been acting really strange lately," Georgie said. "Are you going to tell me what's going on?"

"It's nothing," Alice said unconvincingly.

"Is it Cameron?" Georgie asked. "Has he done something?"

Alice gave a hollow laugh. "Cameron has done nothing except continue to fail to notice me as a potential girlfriend. Not that I care."

"So what is it?" Georgie sat down on the edge of Alice's bed. "Come on Alice, I'm going to find out what it is eventually so you might as well tell me."

Alice sighed and sat up. "It's Allegra Hickman."

"I thought you were getting on pretty good with her?"

"I am!" Alice groaned. "It's just that... you know the other day when I was talking about rollkur... well... Allegra uses it."

Georgie was shocked. "You're kidding me!"

Alice shook her head. "I don't know what to think. I mean, she knows far more about horses than I do and I've learnt so much being her apprentice. I could never have ridden a half-pass or a shoulder-in before she taught me..." Alice took a deep breath, "I know she's the expert, but to me it still seems wrong."

"Why don't you talk to her about it?" Georgie said.

"I did!" Alice said. "You should hear her explaining it, Georgie! The way she talks about rollkur, it all makes perfect sense and I feel like this idiot who knows nothing..."

Alice looked utterly miserable. "Georgie, she's one of the best dressage riders in the world. I'm just a school kid. My opinion doesn't matter – I should just shut up and learn."

"You're not just a kid," Georgie said. "You're a good rider, Alice. You should go with your gut instinct."

Alice looked distraught. "What if my stupid gut is wrong? I could get fired and then I'll fail Tara's class and Allegra Hickman will never speak to me again."

"I can't believe we were looking forward to this term," Georgie groaned. "We must have been crazy."

On Monday afternoon, the minibus dropped Alice at Allegra Hickman's yard at the usual time. Alice headed straight for the stables and was halfway through mucking out the boxes when Allegra arrived.

"You've got the place looking lovely," Allegra said brightly. "Great work!"

"Thanks," Alice replied.

"Listen, I hope you don't mind, but we'll have to skip your lesson today," Allegra said. "I have two new horses arriving tomorrow morning so I need you to prepare two extra boxes. I've got to work three horses myself so I think we're going to run short on time."

"No, no…" Alice said, "that's fine."

Allegra Hickman smiled, "Good. Please tack up Damsel for me and bring her out to the arena."

For the rest of that afternoon, Alice busied herself preparing the loose boxes and tacking up horses. The last horse that Allegra was riding that day was Esprit. Alice had saddled up the big chestnut gelding and handed him over to Allegra then she'd returned to the stables to finish off the last chores of the day, filling hay nets and water troughs.

When she finally finished her duties, Alice headed back out to the arena for her end of the day chat with Allegra.

But Allegra was still giving Esprit his workout. She had Esprit's head jammed into the now horribly familiar outline of the rollkur, the horse's magnificent neck contorted so that his head was rammed to his chest. As Allegra urged the horse to trot, Alice watched the way the horse moved, flinging out his legs in an extravagant and glamorous manner, which looked spectacular at first glance. But upon closer inspection, Alice could see the awful tension in the horse, the stiffened back, the painful set of his neck. Esprit's ears were flat back and a thick froth covered his lips as he fought against the hands that held him so tightly against his will.

Alice didn't know how long Allegra had been riding Esprit like this, but she guessed it had been quite a while as the horse looked exhausted and wet with sweat. Allegra began to ride him in circles and then took him down the long side of the arena, still bending his neck tightly but now also twisting it, first to one side and then to the other as Esprit swished his tail angrily.

And then Alice saw the horse's tongue. In an effort to resist the bit, Esprit must have resorted to thrusting his tongue out of his mouth, but this had only made matters worse. His tongue had now become wedged. It was sticking out of his mouth, pinned beneath the hard press of the bit's metal bar.

Alice stared at Esprit's tongue lolling out like a limp dishrag, covered in foam, dangling from the horse's lips.

It was trapped. Alice watched in horror as the tongue began to turn blue from the pressure.

Allegra didn't seem to notice. She kept Esprit's neck bent in the same cruel, twisted crescent of the rollkur. Alice couldn't sit by and watch this. She had to say something.

"Allegra!" Alice got up and waved to the dressage rider. "Allegra!"

Allegra Hickman pulled her horse from a trot to a halt.

"Yes, Alice? What is it?"

"His tongue! It's stuck under the bit. Look!"

Allegra didn't register what Alice said at first, but then she bent down over her horse's neck and spied the blue tongue hanging from Esprit's lips.

Alice had expected Allegra to be as shocked as she was. She had at least expected the dressage trainer to let go of the pressure on the reins and dismount to attend to her distressed horse.

But Allegra Hickman didn't do either. Completely unfazed, as if she had done it a million times before, she stayed in the saddle and reached out a hand along the horse's neck until she grabbed the numb, blue tongue in her fingers. Wiggling it free of the bit, she shoved the tongue back up into Esprit's mouth. And then, with a thank you nod to Alice, she pushed the horse straight back into a trot, and continued to work him as if nothing had happened.

At that moment, all Alice's self-doubt disappeared. She knew that what she had seen today in the dressage arena was deeply wrong. She knew that the horses were suffering. And she knew she had to do something about it.

"You have to tell Tara."

Back at Badminton House the friends had gathered in Georgie and Alice's room. Alice had filled them in on what had happened at Allegra's and their decision was unanimous.

"Tara is the only person who can deal with this," Georgie insisted. "You've tried talking to Allegra. She won't listen."

"And if you go up against her yourself you could end up getting fired and failing the class," Emily added.

"Tara will know how to handle it," Daisy agreed.

"I don't know," Alice looked nervous. "Georgie, will you come with me?"

"Of course I will."

Alice smiled gratefully. She took a deep breath and pulled herself together with a new resolve.

After dinner that evening, while the rest of the girls walked back down the driveway to the boarding house, Alice and Georgie walked around the quad and up the stairs that led to the Blainford staffroom.

It was late in the day and most of the teachers had gone home, but as luck would have it, Tara Kelly was still there, filling her bag with paperwork.

"Girls!" Tara was surprised to see them. "Who are you looking for?"

"Umm," Alice felt her stomach twist in knots, "Actually, I wanted to talk to you."

Tara shoved the last of the papers into her bag. "Well, come on then," she said heading out into the hall. "I'm on my way to the stables to pick up something from the tack room, come with me and we can talk at the same time."

As they walked the paths that ran between the red brick buildings of the Academy to the stable blocks Alice filled Tara in on everything. She told her teacher about the rollkur, and about her growing doubts as she watched Allegra with the horses, and then the awful episode with Esprit and his trapped blue tongue.

Tara listened in silence with a grave expression on her face.

"And you say that the horse's tongue turned blue?" she asked.

"Totally," Alice said. "Allegra didn't care. She just stuffed it back into his mouth and kept riding."

Tara nodded. They had reached the stable block now, and at the tack room she stopped at the front door. "Right, girls, thank you for bringing this to my attention," Tara said stiffly. "I... I... will give it consideration."

And with that, Tara walked into the tack room and shut the door behind her.

Chapter Twelve

There were the only two Badminton House girls present at Tara's lesson on Monday morning. Daisy was away for the week so she could travel with Seb Upton-Baker to Kansas City for the inter-state polo tournament, and Emily was resting Barclay after the big black Thoroughbred had tracked up lame at last Friday's jumping session.

"Barclay's still not sound," Alice said as she tacked up Caspian. "Emily thought it might get better over the weekend, but it's worse so the vet is coming today to look at him."

Georgie tightened Belle's girth and led the mare out to join Alice who was already mounting up.

"So are you going to Allegra's this afternoon?" Georgie asked.

Alice sighed. "I guess so. Tara didn't say anything to me about not going."

Georgie frowned. "Maybe you could try to explain it to her again?"

"And embarrass myself even more?" Alice groaned. "Tara's probably thinking that I'm totally out of line as it is. I mean, who am I to criticise a world-class rider?"

"You could try talking to Allegra again..." Georgie offered.

Alice shook her head with a flat look in her eyes. "I've only got two weeks left on this apprenticeship and right now Allegra thinks I'm great. All I have to do is keep my head down, work hard and not get involved and I'll get the mark I need to pass into next year's eventing class. So that's what I'm going to do."

The lesson that morning was one of the best that Georgie had ever had. Tara had set up a full jumping course and many of the fences were substantial – there was a spread that measured a metre forty high and wide. Each of the jumps was set up at a tricky angle or a complicated related distance from the last fence so that Georgie really needed to keep her wits about her as she rode.

"Today," Tara said, "I want to put the focus on to flying changes. You're probably accustomed to changing legs so that your horse is on the right canter lead as you go over a fence, but today we'll take it up to a new level."

Tara had constructed the course with a particularly tight turn after the third jump.

"As you take the fence, you need to be thinking about the next jump," Tara explained, "and because it's set at a strange angle you must canter on one leg heading left, and then execute a flying change to turn right without missing a beat to take the jump."

Rather than doing the whole course, Tara drilled the girls through the two fences until they had mastered the change so when the time came to do the whole course the flying change seemed to come naturally to Georgie.

"Keep working on this," Tara advised. "Belle is a very capable mare. I don't think we've seen the full extent of her talent yet."

Despite her underlying concern for Alice, the lesson had put Georgie in a good mood as she headed into the dining hall for breakfast. She'd grabbed a tray and joined the queue and had just ladled a big scoop of scrambled eggs on to her plate when she felt a sharp elbow thrust into her back.

"Oww! Watch it!" Georgie spun around and found she was face-to-face with Kennedy Kirkwood.

"I'm not the one that needs to watch it!" Kennedy said viciously. "I'd be watching my back permanently if I were you! And your front – boyfriend-stealer!"

"Kennedy," Georgie stammered, "I don't know what he's told you, but it was nothing, honestly."

"Nothing?" Kennedy scowled at her. "If it was nothing then why has he broken up with me?"

"What?" Georgie blurted out. "Ohmygod, I'm so sorry!"

Kennedy reached over the cafeteria counter and picked up the scrambled egg ladle and then, with a contemptuous flick of her wrist, spattered the front of Georgie's uniform with scrambled goo.

"You don't know the meaning of sorry." Kennedy

stepped in front of Georgie and took a piece of toast and put it neatly on her tray as if nothing had happened. "But you will. By the time I'm finished with you, you'll wish you'd never come to Blainford."

After the dining-hall incident Kennedy failed to turn up for the afternoon apprenticeship at Dominic Blackwell's yard. This came as a colossal relief to Georgie who had been imagining all the other things that Kennedy might be thinking of throwing at her.

Tuesday came and when the pupils piled into Kenny's minibus after lunch, once again Kennedy was not among them.

"What's going on?" Georgie said to Alice. "Where is she?"

"I wouldn't question it if I were you," Alice told her. "Since Kennedy has declared war on you, I'd just be glad that you don't have to spend the day with her."

Dominic Blackwell was already in the arena when Georgie arrived, riding one of his young horses. The bay horse was a spooky sort and kept baulking at the fills in the jumps, eyes white with terror as it leapt sideways. Georgie watched Dominic Blackwell as he calmly, but firmly, kept the horse on track and ignored its extravagant spooks. He rode it hard at the jumps until eventually the young horse was no longer fretting and was in a steady canter around the fences.

That was the strange thing about Blackwell, Georgie thought. He understood his horses, but when it came to people, it was like his brain was disconnected. He simply didn't know how to be nice – or didn't care to be.

Dominic dismounted and was leading the young bay horse when suddenly it leapt out of its skin and began to snort and piaffe on the spot with panicky excitement.

The horse was being driven wild by the sound of a helicopter. Georgie could hear the unmistakeable thud of the aircraft's rotors whirring as it grew nearer. She assumed the helicopter must belong to a neighbouring farm, and that it was heading across the Blackwell estate.

But the noise of the rotors didn't recede. The sound grew louder and louder and then, like something out of a James Bond movie, a shiny jet black helicopter suddenly appeared over the rooftop of Dominic Blackwell's house.

Hovering for a moment above the stable block, the helicopter seemed to pivot on its axis and then it lowered down out of the sky, right in the middle of Dominic Blackwell's driveway – no more than twenty metres away from the arena.

The young horse was no less disturbed by the sight of the mechanical beast. He was still dancing and fretting uncontrollably, but that didn't stop Dominic Blackwell from throwing the reins to Georgie.

"Hang on to him for me," Dominic said as casually as if he'd passed her his sweater not some berserk half-a-tonne of horse.

The helicopter had landed now and the engine was switched off so that the rotor blades began to slow down. They still created a slight breeze though and the air messed up Dominic's well-crafted sweep of hair as he bent low and ran forward to open the door of the helicopter and let the passengers out.

The first person to emerge from the helicopter was a woman. She greeted Dominic Blackwell and then pointed back to the helicopter, sending him to help the second passenger.

Staying bent over to avoid the rotor blades, the woman walked towards Georgie. She was wearing an expensive-looking black suit and high heels and her jet black hair was tied back in a high ponytail. Her features were undeniably beautiful, cold and haughty, and Georgie recognised her immediately. It was Kennedy's stepmother, Patricia Kirkwood.

Back when Georgie was dating James, Patricia Kirkwood made her position on their relationship quite clear.

"There's a certain calibre of girl that is suitable for a Kirkwood," she had told Georgie back then. "I think James has forgotten that."

Now, once again, Patricia Kirkwood was here to make her message abundantly clear.

"Hello Georgina," Patricia looked Georgie up and down, and her nose wrinkled slightly as if there was an offensive smell in the air and she had just figured out where it was coming from. "I understand that you've been busy this term, keeping yourself occupied with other people's boyfriends."

Stunned by her outspokenness, Georgie was left opening and shutting her mouth without any sound coming out. Patricia Kirkwood turned her back on her and smiled at Dominic Blackwell who was now heading over to join them, having helped Kennedy to duck her way under the rotors.

"Dominic!" Patricia Kirkwood's crystal voice cut through the dying whirr of the helicopter rotors. "How marvellous to see you!"

"Lovely to see you too, Patricia. This is a surprise!"

Patricia and Dominic gave each other air kisses while Georgie and Kennedy both stood and glared at each other.

"I came here to see how my stepdaughter is doing," Patricia Kirkwood said. "She's a very talented rider, but then I'm sure you're well aware of that."

"She takes after her mother," Dominic Blackwell said, meaning to be complimentary. "I mean, her stepmother."

Patricia frowned at him. "Yes, well, thank you, Dominic." She said briskly. "I'm so pleased that

Kennedy has been under your wing this term. The poor darling has suffered some emotional turmoil at school lately. It's been a terrible time for her, just awful. Girls can be so cruel when they are jealous and poor Kennedy is so blessed with looks and talent…" Patricia Kirkwood looked directly at Georgie as she said this.

"Anyway…" Patricia Kirkwood said. "I'll cut to the chase, Dominic. I know that Kennedy very much enjoyed being your head girl, and I would very much appreciate it if you would reappoint her to the role. It would certainly look good on her end-of-term report and I really cannot stress how much this favour would mean to me."

"Patricia, I…" Dominic Blackwell faltered, giving Patricia Kirkwood the chance to drive her point home.

"As you know, Dominic, I am a vigorous sponsor of showjumping. I have been the main benefactor of Hans Schockelmann's string of elite horses for many years now. I have kept my best horse, Tantalus, stabled with him."

Patricia took a deep breath. "However, it's possible

that I might be looking for a new rider to put on Tantalus and some of my other up-and-coming mounts."

Her meaning couldn't have been clearer if she'd taken out a wallet and waved it under Dominic Blackwell's nose.

"I'm sure there's been some misunderstanding, Patricia," Dominic Blackwell was literally rubbing his hands together. He cast a glance at Kennedy who was still standing there looking sullen. "Kennedy is my head girl, and I can assure you that her end of term assessment will be glowing."

"Excellent," Patricia Kirkwood looked at her watch. "I can't stay long, but I'd love a tour of your facilities before I go – that is, if you have the time to show me around?"

"Of course," Dominic Blackwell ran a hand through his luxuriant mane. "Please come this way."

He turned back to Georgie. "Untack the horse and get my next mount ready. You can warm him up for me in the arena."

"I'll do that, Dominic," Kennedy offered. "Georgie can go back to mucking out the boxes."

Dominic Blackwell would have preferred to have Georgie warming up his horse for him. But what choice did he have?

"Georgie," he said, "Kennedy is in charge. You're to do whatever she tells you. "

Georgie's worst nightmare had become reality.

"You are back on dung duty, Parker," Kennedy said, snatching the reins off her. "I warned you, didn't I? Never mess with a Kirkwood!"

Ever since she'd been working for Allegra Hickman, Alice had been in love with Damsel. Of all the horses on the yard, the brown mare was by far her favourite. The mare was an Oldenburg, with the same strong physique, a neck with an impressive topline, and a compact frame with powerful haunches that Caspian possessed. Her paces were so floaty, when she was in motion it appeared to Alice as if Damsel barely touched the ground.

Damsel was only a medium-grade dressage mount and had yet to master the more advanced manoeuvres like passage or pirouettes, but the mare was coming along brilliantly and could do a very nice half-pass and lovely shoulder-ins.

Alice was thrilled when she saw on the blackboard in the stables that she was down to ride Damsel in her lesson with Allegra that afternoon.

"I think this mare is ready for some real work, don't you?" Allegra said as she strode into the arena. In her hands she had a piece of string with a series of knots in it, and she came over to Damsel, talking softly to the mare as she attached one end underneath her belly to the centre of her girth.

"OK, Alice," Allegra said. "Ask Damsel to bend and flex at the poll and drop her head."

Alice did as her trainer asked. She flexed the mare by putting her legs on and putting pressure on the reins until Damsel dropped her head in submission.

"A little more please, make her take her head down further," Allegra said clinically.

Alice tightened her grip until her knuckles were white and asked the mare to lower her head further still. Now Damsel's head was bent right over so that her forehead seemed to almost face the ground below her and her nose was tucked into her chest.

"More!" Allegra said.

Alice looked at her instructor, horrified. "I can't get her any lower than this," she said weakly.

"You can," Allegra corrected her. "You just need to shorten your reins and take a firmer grip. Now do it!"

"I don't think she's comfortable," Alice said. She could hear Damsel's tail swishing, and she could feel the mare resisting her hard, brutal hands against the reins.

"Shorten the reins," Allegra commanded, "Pull her head down. More."

Alice pulled Damsel's head until the mare's chin was virtually wedged into her chest.

"Hold her there," Allegra said. She reached down to the piece of knotted string, and taking the free end she attached this to Damsel's bit. Even if Alice released her hands Damsel's head would remain tucked to her chest.

"OK," Allegra said. "Now take her out on to the outside track of the school and start working her in that frame at a trot, please."

Alice was so shocked it felt like she was moving in a

dream. She did as Allegra told her to. She took the mare out to the edge of the arena and asked her to trot. As soon as they began to move forward into a faster pace, Alice could feel the difference in the mare. She was stiff and her hindquarters seemed to move robotically as if the pressure on her head was causing so much pain that the mare couldn't swing through her back. Her tail kept swishing constantly and her ears were flattened. Alice felt a lump rise in her throat as she heard the mare grinding her teeth against the bit. With each stride she grunted and snorted, unable to breathe through her restricted airways.

None of this seemed to bother Allegra Hickman. "Press her on into a trot!" Allegra commanded. "And now the other rein! Half-pass! And shoulder-in!"

Alice felt a surge of relief when Allegra finally called her back to the centre of the arena.

"I think that's enough of that," Allegra said as she undid the knot on the string. Then she added, "Now, let's get serious."

With a sick punch to her stomach, Alice realised what was happening. Allegra Hickman was not removing the string on Damsel's bit. She was preparing to tighten it.

"Pull her head down again for me," Allegra ordered.

When Alice looked back years later, she would always say that this was the moment that defined her as a professional rider. It is the hardest thing in the world to stand up to an adult when you are young. It is even harder still to tell someone who supposedly knows more than you that they are wrong. But Alice knew she had no choice. She felt Damsel's pain so keenly it was as if her own neck were being twisted to the point of torment. She couldn't be a part of this any longer.

"I'm not doing it," she told Allegra. "It's cruel and I don't see how you can't understand that."

She released the reins, but the string held Damsel's head and kept it bent. "I won't ride her like this. Undo the string now and I'll take her back to the stable."

Allegra Hickman looked at the young girl sat there defiantly in front of her. "Are you kidding me?"

She gave a mocking laugh, as if this was nothing more than a joke to her. But Alice could see that the confrontation had her more shaken than she would admit. Allegra's hands were trembling.

"I have given you the opportunity to be my apprentice,

to learn from one of the masters of dressage and you think you know more than me?" Allegra Hickman's tone was growing harsher by the second.

"You are not an authority on riding!" Allegra's words were drenched in venom. "You have no right to question me, or my methods!"

"No," a voice behind her said. "But I do."

Allegra Hickman turned around. Standing on the sidelines of the arena with the world's most thunderous expression on her face, was Tara Kelly.

Chapter Thirteen

*A*s Tara Kelly strode across the arena towards her, Allegra Hickman made it clear that she was not pleased to have company.

"I wasn't aware you were coming to visit today, Tara," she said with a chill to her voice. "You might have given me a little warning."

"It's an impromptu visit," Tara replied. "I like to check up on my students and see how their placements are going."

She looked at Alice and Damsel. "And right now I'm not entirely happy with what I'm seeing here."

Tara walked past Allegra, ignoring the indignant look from the dressage rider, and went straight up to Damsel and undid the knotted string releasing the mare's chin from her chest.

"I wasn't aware that you were working your horses in rollkur, Allegra," Tara said.

Allegra Hickman went straight on the defensive. "Don't you come here and mess about with my horses and lecture me!" she shook her head in disbelief. "You – the eventer who knows nothing about proper dressage – have come to point out the error of my ways? How dare you judge my schooling!"

"I wouldn't call this schooling," Tara said keeping her cool, "I would call it torture. How is tethering this poor mare's head down like this supposed to achieve a supple, elastic back and neck? This mare could barely move. She was in pain!"

Allegra Hickman had a defiant look in her eyes. "This is how we train young horses these days," she snapped. "Without rollkur no horse can achieve the flashy leg movements that get the top scores. If I gave up my methods I would sacrifice my chances of ever winning another Grand Prix. This is what I have to do if I want to win."

"Riding a horse like that will destroy them," Tara said. "Their bodies aren't meant to bend to extremes."

"I don't expect you to understand," Allegra shot back. "You are ignorant of the top dressage methods."

Tara shook her head. "I don't understand how someone who I once admired and respected could knowingly make her horses suffer just so she can get to the top."

"You think just because they've banned rollkur from the warm-up arenas that the riders aren't still doing it in private?" Allegra said darkly. "Wake up, Tara! This is the real world."

Tara looked at the mare standing beside Allegra Hickman. The mare's breathing had recovered now that Tara had released the knot, but she was still trembling, her coat was wet with sweat.

"This isn't the real world," Tara said, "This is hell."

She looked up at Alice who had been in saddle on Damsel's back the whole time. "Dismount and get your things, Miss Dupree. Your apprenticeship is over."

That day Alice left Allegra's yard for the last time. She didn't say goodbye to her employer – which was fine by her. She had nothing more to say to Allegra Hickman. But she felt a lump in her throat as she said farewell to the horses.

"I'm sorry you had to go through this, Alice," Tara said as they drove out the gates and on to the back roads that led to Blainford. "When you told me about what was happening, I was so shocked, I'm afraid I didn't know how to react. If I'd had any idea that Allegra Hickman was practising rollkur I would never have placed you on her yard. It goes without saying that you will get a pass mark for your final grade this term."

"So what's going to happen now?" Alice asked.

Tara considered this. "It's too late to find you another placement at this stage with only two weeks left in the apprenticeships, so I think the best plan would be for you to help me in the stables for the next fortnight. I'll give you some private cross-country lessons on Caspian and we'll get him up to speed for next year. I think he'll be an excellent sophomore horse for you – he's a bold jumper."

She had expected Alice to be happy about this, but

the girl in the front seat beside her still looked upset. "Is there something wrong, Alice?"

"I didn't mean me. I meant what's going to happen to the horses? What are we going to do about Damsel, the brown mare that I was riding when you came today? She's a really lovely horse and Allegra is going to ruin her."

"Unfortunately that's Allegra's choice," Tara replied. "She can do what she likes in the privacy of her own yard. All I can do is inform the owners of her horses about what I've seen at her stables – and perhaps some of them may choose to take their horses elsewhere for schooling. I'm afraid Allegra is considered to be a top rider and many of her owners will undoubtedly dismiss my concerns and leave them with her at that yard. They want results and they know Allegra will deliver."

"But she's putting those horses through agony!"

"I know," Tara agreed. "Some of the horses will survive her methods – but many others will develop injuries and the damage will eventually make them unrideable. Even the ones who do manage to get through her training will probably have brief lives in the spotlight because their necks and backs won't be able to stand the rollkur for long. Their careers will be short and brutal. "

"I'm never going to ride like that," Alice said, tears running down her cheeks. "I don't care if I don't win. I'll never be like her."

Tara kept her eyes on the road, and gestured at the glove box. "There are some tissues in there," she said. And then she added, "I'm very proud of you, Alice. As far as I'm concerned, you're already a greater horsewoman than Allegra Hickman."

The week that followed Patricia Kirkwood's helicopter entrance brought a whole new nightmare for Georgie. Now that Kennedy Kirkwood had been reinstated as head girl it was becoming horribly clear to Georgie just how little Kennedy actually knew about horses.

Kennedy had grown up being lavished with the very best instructors and horses – Patricia even paid for Hans Schockelmann to fly all the way from Europe to give Kennedy private lessons.

But handling a horse on the ground was an entirely different story. On the Kirkwood estate there were staff to do everything, and even at Blainford Kennedy simply paid other first-years to do her dirty work like mucking out the boxes and pulling manes and tails. As a result she knew virtually nothing about the day-to-day care of her own horse. And on a busy working competition yard she was worse than useless.

Even the most basic tasks like manoeuvring horses into their boxes at the end of the day or tying up haynets in the stalls gave her a total meltdown. Her incompetence didn't escape Dominic Blackwell. But now he was forced to turn a blind eye to keep Patricia happy. "Get Georgie to do it for you," he would tell Kennedy whenever he caught her making a hash of things.

Get Georgie to do it for you. In fact, get Georgie to do everything because you don't even know how to pick out a hoof or rug up a horse. Kennedy was head girl by name alone. Georgie was the one that Dominic Blackwell actually relied upon.

With Kennedy at the helm, the stables lurched from one near-crisis to the next. On Friday afternoon, just when Georgie thought she had got through the week without a disaster, she caught Kennedy trying to mix raw sugarbeet into the horse feeds.

"Kennedy," Georgie was horrified. "You have to soak it in water for two hours first!"

"Oh you always have to be right, don't you? You're such a drama queen!" Kennedy had ignored Georgie's protests as she poured sugarbeet pellets into the tubs.

"I'm serious!" Georgie said. "If you don't soak it first the hard sugarbeet swells in their stomachs – it will kill them!"

Kennedy stopped dishing out the pellets and put the bucket down in a huff. "Fine!" she sniffed, "You do the feeds if you're such an expert."

Georgie took the beet pellets out again carefully and then hunted around the feed room. "Hey! Where's all the sugarbeet that I already soaked last night?" she asked. "It was sitting over there in the red bucket."

Kennedy stiffened. "Oh," she said. "I thought that was something disgusting. I threw it out."

Georgie sighed. "Never mind. I'll give them chaffage instead."

She began to root about in the storage bins, digging out scoops of various feeds and putting together the meals for all the horses. She was mixing up a bin of chaffage and broodmare mix with her bare hands when Kennedy came back in. Kennedy was reading over the contents of a white folder with a gold and blue sash on the cover.

"What's that?"

Kennedy glared at her. "It's for the head girl, not the minion."

She sat down on a feed bin and began to flick through the folder while Georgie continued the grubby task of hand-mixing all the feeds. Georgie read the front of the folder. It was the programme for the upcoming Grand Prix at the Kentucky Horse Park.

Georgie stopped mixing the feed. "Can I please have a look?" she asked.

Kennedy stared at her. "Sure. Take my boyfriend and then take my competition programme!"

Georgie groaned. "Kennedy, I keep telling you it wasn't like that..."

"Oh, whatever!" Kennedy clearly didn't want to

discuss Conrad. She began flicking through the programme. "It's a two-day event," she informed Georgie. "Saturday is the mid-grade classes, and on Sunday they're jumping Grand Prix."

Kennedy turned the page and frowned. "There's a class on the Sunday called Mirror Jumping. Is it like when you jump over a mirror?"

Georgie shook her head. "I've seen them do it at Hickstead. They set up two totally identical showjumping courses – then at the exact same time two riders enter the ring and they both jump against each other. The first one to finish wins."

"Dominic must be entered because he's got a tick beside it." Kennedy sighed. "I suppose he's expecting us to work both days. I can't wait for this apprenticeship thing to be over!"

Georgie's blood suddenly ran cold. She leapt at Kennedy. "Let me see that programme!"

"No!" Kennedy whisked it out of her range. "Your hands are filthy."

"Kennedy!!" Georgie reached out and made a snatch at the programme. "Give it here!"

She had it in her hands before Kennedy could stop her and she flicked to the front of the programme. On the blue sash across the cover the date of the competition was stamped out in gold letters. Saturday the 23rd was Saturday week! The same date as the Firecracker Handicap.

"What difference does it make?" Daisy said. "You're not going to the Firecracker anyway. You've split up with Riley!"

Georgie looked across the dining table at Daisy and resisted the urge to throw her morning porridge at her.

"Firstly," she said, "It's not just Riley's race, OK? Marco is in it too and he used to be my horse and I want to see him run." She paused. "And secondly, I haven't split up with Riley. We are on a break, that's all."

Daisy raised an eyebrow at the other girls sitting with them at the table. Emily and Alice both said nothing.

"A break?" Daisy continued. "And how long has it been since you began this 'break'?" Daisy did air quotes as she said this.

"A month," Georgie admitted.

"Uh-huh," Daisy said. "And how many times have you spoken to him since then?"

"Umm, roughly?" Georgie said.

"Roughly."

"None."

Georgie had called every day but Riley refused to pick up the phone. And, no matter how many messages she left, he wasn't calling her back.

The rule at Badminton House was two phone calls a day. On Saturday Georgie had already exhausted her quota for the day, but she was so desperate to talk to Riley she decided to ignore the rules and resolved to dial him a third time. She was heading out of the room to sneak to the boarding-house phone when Alice came back in and caught her.

"Ohmygod," she shook her head. "Please tell me you aren't about to go and leave another message on Riley's answerphone."

"No," Georgie lied.

Then, suddenly she had a better idea. "No actually, I'm going out."

"What do you mean? Out where?"

"I'm taking Belle for a road hack," Georgie said.

"Oh," Alice said. "I'll come with you if you want. Caspian could do with a hack."

"Sorry, Alice," Georgie said. "I need to go alone."

As she tacked Belle up in the stables, Georgie began to think her plan was crazy. If Riley didn't even want to speak to her over the phone, what made her think that he wanted to see her? But she didn't care any more. She was desperate to tell him how she felt – no matter what happened.

It had been a long time since she'd taken Belle out of the school grounds. The mare had her head held high as they rode through the silver and blue gates of the Academy and out on to the road, her ears pricked forward as she looked around. Georgie kept her on a short contact at first, but after they'd been out on the roads for a while, she relaxed the reins and Belle began to swing along, enjoying the outing. It was a sunny summer day and the Kentucky countryside was glorious.

The fields went on forever, the white plank fencelines merging into one another. Every road seemed to look the same, but Georgie knew the route she was taking. She turned down one back road and then another, past more white plank fencelines and elegant horse farms until she reached the farm with a pale green beaten-up mailbox at the front gate.

As she rode down the driveway of Clemency Farm Georgie realised she might have come all this way for nothing. Riley might not even be here today at his father's stables.

"Hello?" She rode Belle into the yard, but there didn't seem to be anyone around. Then she heard the sound of hoof beats. There was a galloper out on the dirt track at the back of the farm. Dismounting, she led Belle around the back of the stables. Out on the track she could see a rider working his horse around the broad loop of the circuit. The rider was heading away from the stables to the far end of the track. He was a hunched figure, his body bent down low over the horse's withers. The horse he was riding was a chestnut with a white blaze and Georgie recognised him straight away. It was Marco, and that was Riley up there on his back.

As the horse and the rider looped back around the track towards the stables, Georgie wasn't certain if Riley had seen her or not. He stayed motionless on Marco's back, letting the horse run at his own pace. Georgie could tell that he was just breezing the gelding – letting him gallop, but not pushing him to go into top speed. With the race now just a week away he would have a training schedule mapped out to the very last detail and this trackwork would have been meticulously planned.

The track at the back of the Clemency Farm stables was a makeshift affair, not quite full-sized, so Riley had to keep the horse galloping for an extra half a loop to make the right distance. Then, when Marco had passed the furlong post, he slowed the gelding up and began to trot him around the track, doing the full loop to cool him down. He was walking the horse by the time he came around for the second time and dismounted. He had seen Georgie now and she knew it – but he hadn't given her a wave. Suddenly she felt like it had been a ridiculous idea to come here. What had she expected? That Riley would be thrilled to see her?

Finally, the boy led the horse off the track and with Georgie right there waiting at the gate he had no choice but to acknowledge her.

"Hey, Georgie."

"Hey, Riley," she smiled at him. "Marco's looking good."

Riley nodded, "He's going OK."

There was an uncomfortable pause that became an even more uncomfortable silence and then, just when it was unbearable, both of them tried to speak at once.

"I was…"

"Hey…"

"You go ahead," Georgie managed to stammer.

"No," Riley said. "You talk first. You've come here so I'm guessing you've got something to say."

Ever since the day they broke up, Georgie had been rehearsing her lines in her head, thinking of exactly what to say if Riley had ever picked up the phone.

Riley stared at her expectantly. Georgie could feel her heart racing.

"I do have something to say," she paused.

"I... umm... I... I think you should hold Marco back."

"What?" Riley frowned.

"You should hold him back. Let him lose the race," Georgie said.

"You came here to tell me that I should let Marco lose the Firecracker?" Riley shook his head. "That's really funny, Georgie!"

"Not the whole race, obviously!" Georgie said. "But I've been thinking about the Hanley Stakes and the way The Rainmaker beat him that day. Marco was in the lead all the way until the final furlong, right? And then The Rainmaker took him in the home stretch. But that's because Marco didn't know he was coming. If you hold Marco back and let him look that big black stallion in the eye, then Marco will want to beat him. I know he will. If you let The Rainmaker pull away out in front of Marco and then at the last minute let him go, he'll fight back. He'll run him down."

Riley raised an eyebrow. "That's what you came here to tell me?"

Georgie looked down at the ground. "There was some other stuff I was going to say, about being in love with you and all that, but yeah, mostly it was about Marco."

"Oh," Riley said. "Right. Good."

Georgie was kind of hoping he might say something more than that. But Riley just paused then handed Marco's reins over to her. "Here – hold him for a minute. I've got to go and get something."

He returned from the stables with a brown paper envelope in his hand which he thrust at Georgie.

Georgie opened it. Inside she could see a peek of gold-embossed card.

"They're invitations to the owners' enclosure at the Churchill Downs Racecourse," Riley said. Georgie saw the words Firecracker Handicap were emblazoned at the top. The date of the race was also there and sure enough it was next Saturday – the same date as the showjumping at the Kentucky Horse Park.

"I booked them for you ages ago. There are four tickets so you can bring the girls with you," Riley said. "Mom and Dad already have their tickets so you can sit with them."

Georgie up at Riley. "So you still want me to come?"

Riley nodded. "I'm sorry I didn't pick up the phone when you called. I just needed some time to think. But whenever I hear your voice on my answerphone all I can think is how much I miss you. You're my best friend, Georgie."

"You're mine too."

"It really hurt, you know, finding out about you and Conrad."

"It was a stupid mistake," Georgie said, "and I'm so, so, sorry. Is there a chance we can put it behind us?"

Riley raked a hand through his hair. "Yeah, I can do that," he said.

Then he added, "So you'll come and watch me race?"

He noticed the anxious look on her face. "Is there something wrong, Georgie? You don't have other plans that day, do you?"

Chapter Fourteen

Georgie shifted anxiously in her seat and looked out the window of the horse truck. It was still dark outside, the dawn light was only just beginning to seep across the pastures as they approached the Kentucky Horse Park. So far the morning routine had gone like clockwork and they were on schedule to reach the grounds by six am. In the back of the truck Dominic's second-string horses – Banner, The Optimist, Flair and Navajo – were rugged and bandaged for the journey. She had the horses manes plaited and their tails pulled. The tack was organised into labelled sections for each horse and she had the studs ready to fit into their shoes as soon as she unloaded them.

To do all of this in time for the competition today

Georgie had worked until midnight the night before, packing out the truck and grooming the horses. Then she had set her alarm next to a cot bed in the stables, and hunkered down in her jods with a sleeping bag, using her jumper for a pillow. She slept until four am when she had forced herself to get up again and started work once more.

Getting four manes fully plaited in two hours had been hard work, but what other choice did she have? This was the way it had to be if she wanted to watch Riley in the Firecracker this afternoon.

Georgie knew how Dominic Blackwell's mind worked. If she had asked him for the day off on Saturday to go watch her boyfriend race he would never have agreed. Instead, on Friday afternoon, she had phrased her proposition in a way that Blackwell could understand.

"I need a couple of hours off on Saturday afternoon," she said. "I know it's a competition day, but it won't interfere with your riding. I won't leave the showgrounds until one pm and I'll be back again in time to load the horses and take them home. I'll get everything prepared down to the last detail so that the horses are totally ready – Kennedy won't need to do a thing apart from tack a couple of them up for you. You won't even miss me, and I promise that I'll work all of Sunday for the Grand Prix and the Mirror Jumping to make up for it."

"I don't know…" Dominic looked uncertain about losing his best groom, even for an hour or two.

"Please, Dominic," Georgie begged. "Everything will go fine without me. I'll leave written instructions for Kennedy. Saturday is just the mid-grade jumping anyway – it's the Sunday that really matters."

Dominic Blackwell sighed. "All right. You can go. But not until I've jumped in the one-thirty class on Navajo. I want you to warm her up for me."

If Georgie left the Kentucky Horse Park at two she would be cutting it fine to make it to Riley's race. But it could be done. And if that was the deal that Dominic Blackwell was putting on the table, then she should take it.

"Thank you, Dominic," she had replied. "I won't let you down."

The atmosphere at the Kentucky Horse Park that morning was bright and friendly. As this was a mid-grade tournament for the professional riders it was a low-key day. The metre-ten class was now underway but Dominic refused point-blank to ride his horses in it.

"Blackwell doesn't leave the horse truck for less than a metre-twenty," he had pointed out snootily when Georgie had asked him why the horses weren't entered in the competition. "It's beneath me."

Georgie was so over-prepared she actually had a spare half-hour to watch the final riders compete in the metre-ten class before she went back to the truck, finished tacking up The Optimist and vaulted onboard to begin the horse's warm-up.

When her boss emerged from the horse truck in his red jacket and high black boots Georgie was all ready and waiting for him.

Dominic Blackwell looked impressed with Georgie's fine-tuned timing. And when he took The Optimist into the ring and jumped a clear round on the chestnut gelding, he came back to the truck in a good mood.

"He's going nicely today," he said to Georgie, flinging her the reins. "Cool him down for me, will you?"

Georgie couldn't believe how seamlessly the whole day was going. Team Blackwell was a well-oiled machine, even though she was only one doing the work. Kennedy had pretty much done nothing all day, sitting on the back ramp of the truck on a pile of horse rugs in the sunshine reading *Vogue* magazine. She'd had less than no interest in helping – which suited Georgie just fine. The last thing she needed was Kennedy messing things up. Right now, Dominic Blackwell's horses were all performing brilliantly, he was scooping up the prizes in every category and for once he didn't seem to have any complaints about anything.

At one o'clock, Georgie tacked up Navajo for her jumping class. The mare was looking spectacular. Georgie had really worked hard on her mane and she had a perfect row of well-sewn plaits. She had bandaged her legs with white bandages and put on a matching white saddlecloth.

As she mounted up, Georgie looked at her watch. For the next twenty minutes, Georgie would ride the warm-up on the mare and then, as soon as she handed her over to Dominic Blackwell, she would grab her bag, give Kennedy her list of instructions and climb into Kenny's waiting pick-up truck and high-tail it to Churchill Downs for The Firecracker Handicap.

It was hard to focus on warming up Navajo when all she could think about was the clock ticking and the fact that she couldn't wait to leave. Georgie had to really force herself to concentrate on working the mare in. She did canter work to loosen up, then brought her back and did lots of transitions from canter to walk and even a few rein-backs to keep Navajo on her toes. Finally, she popped the mare over the practice jump a couple of times until she felt confident that the horse was ready.

The clock said one twenty-five. She rode the mare on a loose rein back to the horse truck. As she got closer she could see the red pick-up truck. Kenny was there waiting for her, just like he'd promised he would be. And Dominic Blackwell was waiting too.

"Ah, Georgie, excellent!" he said as she vaulted off and handed him Navajo's reins. "How is she feeling?"

"She's warmed-up," Georgie replied. "I'm just going to grab my things now. I'll be back here by five."

Dominic Blackwell stuck out his bottom lip and frowned. "Err, no," he said. "No, I don't think so."

Georgie did a double-take. "What do you mean?"

"I've changed my mind," Dominic Blackwell said. "I still have two more classes this afternoon so I'd prefer it if you stayed."

Georgie felt her heart slamming against her chest, pounding hard and fast. He had to be kidding!

"But Dominic!" She struggled to control the anxiety in her voice. "We discussed this yesterday. I planned everything around this. You said if I did everything that I could go!"

"Did I?" Dominic Blackwell said airily. "Well, as I said, I've changed my mind."

There was the click of a car door as Kenny got out of the pick-up truck. He'd heard Georgie's cries of protest and realised that something was wrong. At the back of the horse truck, Kennedy had risen from her comfy position on the horse rugs to see what was going on.

"You made a promise." Georgie was outraged. "I've

got everything running perfectly. You have to let me go."

"Firstly," Dominic Blackwell raised a silencing hand to her, "I don't expect my grooms to raise their voices to me, Georgie. And secondly, I don't have to do anything. I want you here – so you're staying."

"But you don't even need me!" Georgie tried to appeal to Dominic, "Kennedy can cover for me."

"Don't be ridiculous!" Dominic snapped, "Kennedy is a waste of space! I need a proper groom!"

"Hey!" Kennedy said. "I'm standing right here!"

"Oh, wise up, Kennedy," Dominic turned to her. "Despite the fact that you are as useless as a pet rock you're still getting a pass mark for your apprenticeship, your stepmother has taken care of that. But let's not kid ourselves here – you're not head girl material."

"I've got the horses all ready, Dominic," Georgie insisted. "It's only two classes this afternoon. Even Kennedy can handle that!"

Dominic shook his head. "Blackwell doesn't approve," he said firmly. "You're staying, Georgie. That's final."

"No," Georgie said. "It isn't."

She jumped up the steps of the horse truck and grabbed her bag off the kitchen bench. Then she grabbed the handwritten note that was lying beside it and thrust this at Kennedy.

"Here are your instructions. The next class is at three – you'll need to have Flair tacked up for that."

"What are you doing?" Dominic Blackwell's eyes widened. "I told you, Georgie, you're not leaving."

"Really?" Georgie said stomping towards Kenny's pick-up, "Then why are my feet walking in this direction?"

"Georgie!" Dominic Blackwell shouted after her. "If you go now that's it! Blackwell will not stand for it! Blackwell will fail you!"

Georgie stopped in her tracks. She turned back around, her whole body trembling. "Well, go ahead!" she said. "Georgie doesn't care. Georgie is outta here!"

And with that, she threw her bag on to the back of the pick-up and clambered onboard. "Let's go, Kenny," she said. "Take me to Churchill Downs."

Georgie had never seen a racetrack on race day before. In her mind, she'd imagined it would be like Keeneland Park on those mornings when she'd ridden trackwork with Riley. But this was nothing like that. This was racing at full throttle, loud and glamorous. Instead of old jerseys and jeans, the jockeys wore the brightly coloured silks that denoted their stables, and their horses, also dressed in their stable colours, were led by handlers as they paraded in the birdcage beside the track. Thousands of spectators crammed into the stands around the concourse, all hollering and waving their tickets in the air as the horses galloped around the track and came down to the wire of the finish line.

The race-goers were dressed to the hilt and the best dressed of all were gathered on the fifth floor of the grandstands. This was the famed 'Millionaires Row' – the most exclusive private seating area in the whole of Churchill Downs. Here, the rich and the famous rubbed shoulders with royalty. Kenny had led Georgie here after a quick pit stop at the ladies loo where she had got changed in a cubicle, wiggling out of her Blainford uniform and pulling on the fabulous yellow Chanel sundress that Alice had kindly lent her again. Kenny, on the other hand, was still in his usual attire – a pair of dirty old Wrangler jeans, and a ripped plaid shirt.

"It's OK," he said to the security guard on the entrance as he handed him the ticket. "I'm not coming in. This is for the young lady."

He gave Georgie a grin. "You go ahead and have fun. Millionaires' Row ain't my scene. Riley needs me down at the stables."

Have fun! Georgie would far rather be down at the stables too. The room was swarming with women in brilliantly coloured cocktail dresses and enormous hats, and men dressed in sharp suits. Some were in top hats and morning suits like they wore in the pictures she'd seen of the races at Ascot. The room was buzzing with energy and excitement as they drank champagne and sat at tables with waiters hovering around them offering food on silver trays.

"Georgie!" She heard her name being called above the noise of the crowd and then saw Alice waving frantically at her. She began to edge her way gently through the crowded room, trying not to bump into the waiters who were circulating with champagne and platters of canapés.

Alice, meanwhile, was working her way towards Georgie, but she had been sidetracked by a waiter carrying a tray laden with dainty miniature hotdogs.

"You're only supposed to take one, miss," the waiter was insisting as Alice grabbed three at once.

"Are you kidding me?" Alice pulled a face. "Have you seen the size of these things? I'll need to eat like a dozen, just to make one normal hotdog. I'm not following you around all day!"

She turned to Georgie. "This place is the best! Come on, we've got a table beside the balcony. We've got fab seats. We're sitting right behind a table that belongs to the Bulgarian crown prince and on the other side is an Arab sheik – they've both got a horse in the same race as Riley."

Daisy and Emily both leapt up with joy when Georgie arrived.

"Where have you been?" Emily called out. "We were getting worried!"

Beside the girls, a man in a very smart dark suit and tie stood up to greet her too.

"Georgie," John Conway smiled. She had never seen Riley's dad dressed up before and he didn't look entirely comfortable. "I don't feel right in this monkey suit," he said running a finger around the neck of his shirt to loosen it. "I shouldn't be up here with the fancy pants. I should be down at the stables with Riley getting that horse of his ready to run. I've been trying to convince Mary-Anne to let me leave—"

"John Conway!" The woman next to him shook her head. "Stop being foolish. Riley knows what he's doing and he's got Kenny to help him. He doesn't need you getting underfoot. You're going to stay here and enjoy yourself if it kills you!"

The woman gave Georgie a broad smile. "It's lovely to meet you, honey, I've heard so much about you. I'm Mary-Anne Conway, Riley's mother."

"It's great to meet you too," Georgie said. "I'm sorry I was running late…"

"Not at all," Mrs Conway said. "The race is another fifteen minutes away – you're just in time. We should head out on to the balcony."

She handed Georgie a pair of binoculars. "You're

gonna need these – we're up so high above the course you could get a nosebleed from the altitude!"

Out on the balcony, the crowds were beginning to gather. Georgie, Alice, Daisy and Emily grabbed a spot near the railing that gave them a clear view out over the track. They were directly in front of the finishing post. Georgie peered down through her binoculars. The track was still empty at the moment, but any minute now the jockeys would be bringing their horses out.

"What colour silks is Riley wearing?" Emily asked.

"The Clemency Farm colours are royal blue with white diamonds on the sleeves," Georgie told her.

The atmosphere on the balcony was getting tense as the race grew closer, but that didn't stop Alice from hunting down a waiter and commandeering a tray of meringues. "These are just soooo yummy!" she grinned through a mouthful of strawberries and cream. "I love it here! Did I mention how much I love it here?"

Georgie was about to take a second meringue off the tray when the fanfare to announce the next race played over the loudspeaker.

"Welcome back to the racing here at Churchill

Downs!" the announcer said. "This is the sixth race, The Firecracker Handicap, and we are about to get underway in just five minutes. And here the horses come!"

There was more musical fanfare and then two grey horses, the 'outriders', emerged. These horses accompanied the racehorses and were ridden by men in red hacking jackets and velvet hard hats. Following the outriders were the racehorses themselves. Georgie marvelled at the beauty of the horses as they stepped out lightly on to the sandy loam of the track. They were Thoroughbreds, sleek and gleaming, bays and chestnuts mostly. All the horses looked amazing, but there was one horse who stood out from the others. He was enormous – a jet-black horse with a rider in red and gold silks and the number twelve on his blanket. Georgie knew straight away that this must be him – The Rainmaker – the favourite to win the Firecracker today.

"The Rainmaker looks good," John Conway said darkly. "He's put on some muscle since I last saw him. Maybe that's a good thing – or maybe not. Maybe he'll be too heavy today to go the distance."

"What position has he drawn?" Mary-Anne Conway wanted to know.

"Near the barrier," her husband replied. "Riley is on the outside of him. He needs to keep out of his way and keep an eye on him at the same time. The Rainmaker will be the one to watch all right."

More horses began to pour out on to the track now and the announcer began rattling off names, "Master and Commander, Bullet Proof, Ace of Diamonds, and Regal Rival..."

At the mention of the last name the Bulgarian Prince raised his hands in applause and the woman standing next to him with a giant fascinator on her head, began to shriek and applaud.

"Look!" Alice pointed out to the track. "There's Riley!"

Georgie looked down at the track below them. She could see his royal blue silks with the white diamonds, and Riley strapping on goggles to prepare for the race and keep the mud from the horses' hooves out of his eyes. By the look of Marco though, there wouldn't be many horses in front of him – Georgie had never seen the chestnut gelding in such amazing shape. His muscles rippled in the Kentucky sunshine. His coat had the sheen of a precious metal and his head was held erect as he walked around the track like a cat on hot coals.

"I can't believe that's Marco!" Emily breathed. "He looks amazing."

"He's not Marco," Alice held up the race card to show the others. "He's running under his proper racing name – Saratoga Firefly!"

"Well I'm not yelling that out," Daisy said. "I'm just going to call out Marco."

"The horses are lining up behind the barrier," the commentator's voice was tense. "Number thirteen is refusing to go into the gates..."

"That's Marco!" Emily said.

"Typical," Daisy groaned. "He always has to be the one to cause trouble!"

"No!" Alice said, "Look, he's gone in. It's OK."

The horses were all in the gates and a silence fell over the track. The silence settled into a tense hush and then the air cracked as the metal gates flew open and the horses surged forward. All except for Marco. Instead of breaking at the gates, the chestnut gelding went straight up in a panic-stricken rear. As the other horses leapt forward Riley was struggling with a horse up on his hind legs. The race was on and they had been left behind.

Chapter Fifteen

Come on, Riley, Georgie's hands were shaking as she trained her binoculars on the barrier. *Get him down!*

The roar of the crowd around her was deafening, but all Georgie could hear was the pounding of the blood in her ears as she kept her eyes on the chestnut horse still stuck inside the gates. Out on the track the rest of the pack were already five lengths ahead.

Riley had convinced Marco to put all four hooves back down on the ground, but they were still inside the gates.

"C'mon!" Georgie whispered. It was as if Marco heard her because at that moment he shot from the barrier! They were off!

Riley pressed the Thoroughbred on, instantly picking up the stride, standing in his stirrups in a crouch above

Marco's withers, his eyes trained on the backsides of the galloping horses ahead.

Marco's moment of terror in the barriers was now behind him. He hated to be at the back of the pack and all he wanted was to catch up to the others. He threw himself forward into the gallop, his strides eating up the ground. By the first furlong marker the horses were eight lengths ahead of him, but by the second furlong there were just a couple of lengths between him and the stragglers at the rear of the pack.

Riley was doing all he could to urge Marco on, fighting for each stride as he moved the chestnut gelding closer, edging up on the field.

They began to pick off the stragglers one horse at a time, ducking and weaving their way through the ranks, passing the jockeys and their mounts who fell back as they failed to match the ferocious speed of the pack.

Georgie kept her binoculars trained directly on the little chestnut gelding as he fought his way past one horse after another, his strides relentless as he accelerated to reach the middle of the field.

By the time the horses powered into the final turn

and began to head down to the home straight Riley and Marco had made an incredible comeback. They were right up there near the front with just seven horses ahead of them.

"Marco must be exhausted," Emily said, biting her lip, her knuckles white as she gripped her ticket in her fist. "He's run too hard to make it this far. He won't be able to keep up with the pace in the final stretch."

"Don't give up on him yet," Georgie said softly. "That horse is far too stubborn to know when he's beaten."

Riley was bent down low over Marco's neck and the little chestnut began to really flatten out, his strides coming even faster as he charged his way straight through the field ahead of him.

"Here he comes!" John Conway shouted out. "He's doing it!"

They were in the home stretch now and the little chestnut was right up beside the leaders. In a single stride he overtook the Ace of Diamonds and was gaining on The Rainmaker.

"Go, Marco! Go!" John Conway shouted. But just as quickly as the gelding began his run, he seemed to slow down again. He was alongside The Rainmaker, but it looked like he wasn't able to get past him to get his nose out in front.

"He's stalled," Daisy was aghast. "He's too tired, he can't make the run, they're going to overtake him!"

"No!" Georgie shook her head. "He's not tired. He's playing with him!"

Riley was riding it just the way they'd planned! He was holding Marco back and letting him get a good look at his opponent.

Georgie watched through the binoculars as the chestnut gelding held stride, running neck-and-neck with The Rainmaker. She saw Marco look the big black horse right in the eye. And then, once Riley was certain that Marco had got a good, hard look at his rival, Riley let him go.

This time Marco didn't hesitate. He put on a burst of speed, faster than anything Georgie had ever seen him produce before, and suddenly his strides seemed to quicken to double-time. As he drove forward The Rainmaker was left in his wake. For a half-a-furlong the valiant Ace of Diamonds tried to keep up and match his pace, but then he too fell away, and as they came down to the winning post it was Marco all the way. No one could even touch him as Riley and the little chestnut gelding that no one had ever wanted, the horse that Georgie had bought for a hundred and fifty bucks, crossed the finish line at the famous Churchill Downs to win the Firecracker Handicap by five lengths!

Georgie's throat was choked with emotion and her heart was pounding as she ran down the entrance to the winner's circle.

Standing in the centre lawn, with the camera flashes popping around them, were Marco and Riley. The jockey gave her a wave and Georgie forgot all about the crowds and the TV cameras as she ran to meet them.

"You did it!" She had tears in her eyes as she looked up at him. "You rode it perfectly!"

Riley grinned down at her. "It was just like you said, Georgie! I pulled up alongside The Rainmaker and I let Marco really eyeball him. I could just feel him boiling with fury underneath me. He couldn't stand the thought that this jumped-up giant horse was gonna beat him. After that, all I needed to do was let him go!"

As if to confirm this, Marco gave a snort and stomped a hoof emphatically against the turf beneath him.

Later, Riley would say that Marco took the win in his stride. It was as if the little chestnut always knew he was destined for greatness.

"It just took everyone else a while to realise how special he was," Riley told Georgie.

Georgie shook her head. "Not you," she said. "You saw it in him straight away. You believed in him when no one else did."

Winning the Firecracker didn't change Marco. He was as difficult as he'd ever been. When a reporter and photographer from the *Lexington Herald* came down to the stables to take a picture after his great victory Marco tried to bite the photographer's lens and then turned his rump to the door and refused to turn back round again.

"He's having trouble coming to terms with stardom," Riley told the reporter. "Give him a while to get used to it."

Throughout the celebrations that had followed the race, Georgie put her own troubles aside, but that evening, as Riley gave the girls a lift back to the Academy, she finally confessed what she had done.

"Dominic was being a total jerk," Georgie said. "He wouldn't let me leave. I had no choice but to quit."

Riley was shocked. "You never told me you had work today. Why didn't you say something?"

Georgie shook her head. "I couldn't tell you. I felt so bad about letting you down all the time lately and I really, really wanted to see you ride."

"So you got yourself fired?"

"It was worth it," Georgie was adamant. "Watching you win the race on Marco meant far more than some dumb apprenticeship."

Riley shook his head. "But when Blackwell gives you a fail mark and you get kicked out of the cross-country class again, then what?"

Georgie had been trying not to think about this. She'd been trying to convince herself that it didn't matter that she would once again be turfed out of Tara Kelly's class.

"Maybe you could go and apologise to him?" Alice offered. "There's always a chance he'd take you back. He still has the big competition tomorrow and right now he's stuck with Kennedy as his groom. That's gotta suck."

"I thought you said he was riding today?" Riley asked.

"It's a two-day event," Georgie clarified. "Today was the mid-grade. Tomorrow it's the Grand Prix and the Mirror Jumping."

"So he's saving his best horses for tomorrow?" Daisy asked.

"Alice is right," Emily said. "You should go and beg for your old job back."

Georgie shook her head. "Blackwell's way too arrogant for that."

"So you're just going to give up??" Riley said. "You're going to let Blackwell win? I don't know how that guy can bear to look in the mirror the way he treats his grooms…"

"Ohmygod!" Georgie's eyes widened. "Riley! You're right!"

"I am?" Riley frowned. "About what exactly?"

Georgie felt her heart racing. She still had a chance to ace her apprenticeship – and prove herself to Dominic Blackwell. But to do it, she'd have to put her all her skills on the line.

Chapter Sixteen

Dominic Blackwell wasn't a man to admit when he was wrong. Certainly he would never have actually swallowed his pride and apologised to anyone – especially a lowly groom. All the same, he had to concede that he regretted firing Georgie Parker.

Without his head girl, his Sunday morning at the Kentucky Horse Park had been a disaster.

Kennedy Kirkwood had proved herself to be one hundred percent useless as a groom. She had failed to plait a single mane, didn't know how to put studs in a horse shoe, couldn't attach a martingale properly and not once but twice she tacked up entirely the wrong horse so that Dominic had been forced to withdraw from his classes.

If it weren't for the fact that Kennedy Kirkwood's stepmother had promised him sponsorship he would have fired her ten times by now.

Of all the useless girls he'd had through the Blackwell stables she was without a doubt the worst he'd ever endured.

Not a patch on Georgie. He thought with annoyance. Georgie had been the best groom he'd ever had – able to anticipate his every need, and a good little rider to boot. He'd trusted her to warm his horses up for him – something that he had never truly done with the others. And how did she repay him? By running off to watch her boyfriend ride a race – just when he needed her! Well, he would teach her a thing or two about loyalty. That girl would be receiving a big, fat F on her end-of-term assessment papers when he filled them in tomorrow.

The warm feeling of revenge cheered Dominic Blackwell up a little and he even managed a smile as he climbed down the stairs of the horse truck.

"How much time do we have?" he asked Kennedy.

Kennedy looked up from bandaging Cardinal's legs. "Until what?"

Blackwell's good humour disappeared instantly. "Until... I... am... due... in... the... ring... you... clot!" He ground the words out through gritted teeth.

"No need to get grumpy at me," Kennedy sniffed. "You can read a programme, can't you? Why don't you figure out when you're supposed to be in there?"

If looks could kill, Blackwell would have murdered Kennedy on the spot. As it was, he decided that there was no point in engaging in a battle with the girl. All he had to do was get through the final class this afternoon. He would be riding all three of his best horses – Maximillion, Cardinal and Polaris – in the Mirror Jumping. His losing streak that morning had been depressing, but that was behind him now. Even Kennedy couldn't mess this up for him. Blackwell had done the studs, sorted the martingales himself and checked the tack. His three mounts were ready and waiting.

Dominic Blackwell intended to take out first, second and third place with the best times of the day. All he had to do was keep his mind on the task and try and survive with this twit of a groom for a few hours more.

Back in the horse truck he checked the schedule. The

Mirror Jumping was about to begin in ten minutes. Blackwell had walked the course already, but since he wasn't due to ride for another half an hour he decided to watch the first round before he mounted up and began his warm-up.

As he ran down the steps of the truck he threw a glance at Kennedy who was struggling to bandage Maximillion's legs.

"I'll be riding Maximillion first," he told her. "Bring him to me in ten minutes."

"Shall I..." Kennedy began to speak but Dominic cut her off.

"No!" he said. "Just bring me my horse, OK? That's all I'm asking you to do – even you can't mess that up!"

The grandstand was totally packed that afternoon as the first two horses entered the arena.

"Welcome to Mirror Jumping here at the Lexington Kentucky Horse Park!" The announcer, Jilly Jones, told the crowd. "For those of you who have never seen this event before you are in for a treat. This is an open tournament where the jumps are set at a maximum height of a metre forty. As you can see, two courses have been set up: side-by-side mirror images of each other. Each rider will go into their own matching arena to jump-off against the clock and each other. The first to make it over the line with the least rails down wins their round. So let's welcome our first two competitors today: Penny Simpson on Rembrandt and Daniel Deans on Courtesan!"

In the arena, the two riders and their horses began to canter around and warm up, and then, on the judges orders, they lined up ready to begin. The bell rang and both horses sprang forward.

"Over the first fence and they are both neck-and-neck," Jilly Jones told the crowds. "But look at Daniel Deans taking the lead! He is faster on the turn into fence number two and as they jump the third jump he's out in front of Penny. Oh dear! She's had a rail down at the third fence..."

On the sidelines, Dominic Blackwell watched the two riders in the ring with a technical eye. He saw every move they made – the way that Daniel Deans cut the corner at jump nine to shave another second off his time and still managed to fit in two strides in front of the jump, and the way Penny Simpson lost even more ground to him coming through the triple combination.

As he watched, Dominic Blackwell felt an unexpected pang of nerves. He had been so distracted by horse-shoe studs and martingales when he walked the course, he hadn't really been paying attention. He was ill-prepared for this round and instead of knowing the tricks and turns that would reduce his time, he would be riding this event today by the seat of his pants.

Nevermind, he told himself, *Blackwell is the master of Mirror Jumping. Watching these two fumble around the course will be ample study for me.* The trick after the treble, Dominic decided, was to keep your horse reasonably straight to take the next jump, a green upright fence, and from there you needed to go around to the right of the orange jump and then you'd be lined up to take the last fence, a solid parallel, in a nice, clean three strides for a text book round.

He watched as Daniel Deans crossed the line ahead of his opponent by almost two seconds.

"Daniel's win puts him through to the scoreboard with one minute thirty-three," the announcer said. "It will now be a matter of wait-and-see whether his time is good enough to put him in the final placings by the end of the competition."

Kennedy stood holding Maximillion's reins when Dominic Blackwell returned.

"He's ready," she insisted.

"We'll see about that!" Blackwell said, anxiously double-checking the tack before he mounted up and took his horse to the warm-up arena.

The Mirror Jumping was an open amateur class and Blackwell loathed having common riff-raff in the warm-up arena getting in his way. Still, he had to concede that this 'wild-card' factor was a real crowd pleaser. Throwing in a few rough diamonds to compete against the slick professionals amused the spectators.

By God, this is a particularly motley assortment! Blackwell thought as he trotted Maxi around and then pressed the stallion into a canter to pop him over the practice jump.

There was one horse that he liked the look of – a very elegant bay that he glimpsed nearby. This horse seemed a cut above the rest and Blackwell was pleased when he saw the rider take the bay through towards the main arena. This was clearly his competition: the good-looking bay against his own handsome grey Maximillion. This would be a fitting spectacle for the crowds in the stands.

As he entered the arena behind the bay he looked at the rider. She wore a black jacket and black velvet hard hat and he could see a single blonde braid poking out beneath her helmet. There was something distinctly familiar about her. If only she would turn around so he could see her face…

"Let's give a big Kentucky Horse Park welcome to our next two competitors," Jilly Jones' voice came crisp and clear over the Tannoy. "We've got a real wild-card on our hands here. A last-minute entry and she's got the toughest draw of the competition, facing one of the top riders in the whole country. So let's give a big Kentucky welcome to our next two riders – Grand Prix champion Dominic Blackwell on the mighty Maximillion,

and our contender, Georgie Parker on the Blainford
Academy mare Belladonna!"

In the arena, Georgie heard Belladonna's name being
called over the Tannoy and felt an electric thrill run
through her.

Riley and the others thought her plan was inspired,
and of course they'd offered to help. They had returned
to Blainford at dawn with the horse truck, and arrived
at the Kentucky Horse Park early to place their last-
minute entry in the Mirror Jumping.

Georgie knew the ropes from her years on the circuit
with her mum. There would undoubtedly be a scratching
today – there was always at least one rider who failed
to turn up or had a lame horse. She'd put her name
down as soon as the registration tent opened and sure
enough, at midday when she went back to check, the
course secretary informed her that she would be able
to compete.

"There's just one thing," the secretary had said and
winced. "I hope this won't put you off, but the opening

we've got is up against one of the most seasoned professionals in the competition. Dominic Blackwell's got three horses entered, so he dominates the line-up as you can imagine. Let me see... ah, yes. We've put you down to ride against him on his first horse of the day – Revel's Maximillion."

Georgie felt the knot of nerves in her stomach grow tighter. This was exactly what she'd been hoping for. "Not a problem," she said. "What time do I ride?"

For the rest of the day Georgie had managed to stay well clear of her former boss. Her focus had been on walking the course no less than three times so that she knew the jumps inside out and back to front. Meanwhile, Alice and Riley had prepared Belle, acting as her grooms and giving Georgie space to think about the task.

Now, in the arena at last, she was ready to go head-to-head with her rival.

As the two riders began to circle their horses around their matching arenas, Dominic Blackwell was openly glaring at Georgie. She could feel his stare burning through the back of her riding helmet as she cantered around to settle Belle into her stride. When they lined their horses up on identical start lines facing the grandstand Blackwell accosted her. "What the blazes are you doing here?" he growled.

"Gee, Dominic," Georgie gathered up her reins and held Belle at their line. "First you tell me off for leaving – and now you don't seem happy that I've come back!"

Dominic didn't get a chance to respond. The buzzer was counting down: five-four-three-two-one-go!

Georgie immediately pushed Belle forward into a canter, putting into play everything she had been taught by Tara from the outset.

Rule number one: hit a rhythm. Just like at school, Georgie was counting the strides out loud as she settled the mare in to take the first fence, a simple red and white upright.

This was no training session, though, and Belle knew it. The thousands of spectators in the grandstands had given the mare a shot of adrenalin and Georgie found it hard to hold her steady. They reached the first jump in a rush and Georgie got left behind when the mare took off too soon. They cleared the jump but the landing was rough and it took Georgie a stride or two to pull herself together. Casting a quick glance across at her opponent she could see that Blackwell was edging ever so slightly ahead. Maxmillion had big strides, which meant that on the straight lines and open stretches of cantering between the fences he was bound to beat them. To match the big grey, Belle and Georgie would have to ride smarter and tighter, taking advantage of the turns and cutting corners to get ahead.

On the second fence, however, Georgie had already lost two strides to recover her position and by the time she looked to the next jump it was too late to go in tight and she had to settle for a wider angle. She was annoyed, but it was better to clear the second jump than to take a crazy risk and drop a rail.

Put it behind you and look to the next fence, she told herself.

Blackwell, meanwhile, had taken full advantage of her sloppy start and was cantering on boldly between the fences. By the time they reached jump number three he was clearly in the lead and as Georgie took off he was already landing on Maximillion and was away to jump number four.

In the grandstands the crowd were cheering wildly. Blackwell was putting in a star turn to impress the crowds. Maxi, who always jumped well in front of an audience, was clearing the fences with air to spare and snorting like a steam train after each effort, his huge bounding strides making the horse look twice the size that he actually was.

Belle wasn't anywhere near as big-striding as the mighty grey. But what she lacked in dramatics she made up for in speed and grace. Belle's distinct advantage over Blackwell's stallion was her intensive morning schooling over tight fences. At fence five the crowd gasped as she jumped and then took only one stride before turning like a cutting horse and taking a hard left to put in two very nippy strides for fence six. The manoeuvre was a vital one – it destroyed Maxi's lead and suddenly Georgie was right back on Dominic's tail again. There was a long canter in to fence number eight and Maximillion ate the ground up with his strides to gain more of a lead again. By the time they were over fence nine the stallion had a whole length on Belle. Both horses were still clear!

Jilly Jones was beside herself with excitement. "There hasn't been more than a horse length between these two riders all this time and as they come into fence number ten watch the way Georgie Parker cuts in tight on that corner and takes the jump at a very sharp angle! She has regained crucial seconds and now she is neck-and-neck with Dominic Blackwell!"

Georgie's heart was racing as she powered down stride by stride through the treble. Clear and over. And then three more strides, over, and three more and they were done. But so was Dominic and he was in the lead! Georgie could feel her chances slipping away.

Coming in to the second to last fence, Georgie took a deep breath. The fence was a plain green upright. Every other rider so far today had taken it straight, but Georgie was looking for the advantage, doing what Tara had taught her to do. And right now, against the big-striding Maximillion her best chance was to make a move that no one could possibly anticipate.

"It's the penultimate fence," Jilly Jones told the crowd, "and Georgie Parker seems to have misjudged her angle into this green upright rather badly I'm afraid. She is almost side-on to the fence and coming in fast!"

But Jilly Jones was wrong. Georgie had taken exactly the line she was planning to take into the upright. The angle was tight, but not impossible. Not for Belle. The mare came in and hesitated for brief moment, but Georgie put her legs on. "Go!" she told the mare. "Get over it!"

Belle gave a grunt and launched herself at the green upright. She arced up and over, but as soon as she landed on the other side she was on a collision course with a large potted conifer standing at the side of one of the jumps. As the crowd held their breath, Georgie turned hard, avoiding the crash. Then, in the very next stride, she put her left leg up to the girth and her right leg back as she cornered hard once more, asking the mare for a flying change. Belle swapped legs like a pro. They were at the final fence now, and because of the crazy stunt they had just pulled they were coming in at a totally different angle than anyone had ridden before.

"Georgie Parker has completely changed the game!"

Jilly Jones was hysterical on the Tannoy. "She has taken a wild angle on that green upright and cut inside to make her approach to the final jump – remarkable riding! She's regained her ground. Ladies and gentlemen, we are in for a photo finish!"

Georgie was in mid-air over the last fence when she finally allowed herself a sideway glance at Dominic Blackwell. He was jumping too!

From the moment Belle landed, Georgie was kicking on. Beneath her she felt the mare respond instantly, flattening out to a gallop, her strides stretching out for the finish line. Georgie no longer worried about style or technique – she was riding like a race jockey the way Riley had taught her – high in her stirrups, arms pushing Belle on as she rode the mare in desperation to cross the line.

Through the finish flags they swept, the roar of the crowd in their ears. But who were they cheering for? Who had it been at the final wire?

Chapter Seventeen

"Ahead by a nose from the mighty Maximillion!" Jilly Jones was jubilant. "Georgie Parker takes it!"

Disbelief was written all over Dominic Blackwell's face as he left the arena. Beaten by his own ex-groom! For a man who lived for the roar of the crowds to taste humiliating defeat in public like this was like sipping poison. He was beyond bitter – he was livid!

"Dominic!"

Georgie was riding towards him, but Blackwell turned his back on her and carried on. How dare she approach him now, after what she had just done?

"Dominic, wait!" Georgie was insistent. Blackwell halted Maximillion, holding the grey stallion back from Georgie's mare. They were alone together, just the two of them in the wings of the stadium, and Georgie suddenly felt very small beside this man on the enormous grey Holsteiner.

"Well?" Dominic stared at her imperiously. "What do you want?"

"It's about my apprenticeship," Georgie said.

"Oh," Blackwell said. "If you want to discuss your mark, then you've got perfect timing. As it happens I have just revised your score. It's no longer an 'F'... it is a 'double F minus'!"

Georgie had known he wouldn't take losing well, but even she was surprised by the vitriol.

Blackwell glared at her. "You ran out on me, Georgie. Abandoned your post! Well, this is your punishment."

Georgie seemed remarkably unmoved by Blackwell's melodramatic posturing.

"Here's the thing, Dominic," she said. "If you want revenge then you can fail me. But if you do that then everyone will assume that you did it out of spite because I beat you today. Word will get out that you're holding grudges against fourteen-year-old girls – not exactly the look that you want for your sponsors and adoring fans."

Dominic Blackwell realised that the girl had a point.

"So what do you want?" Blackwell said. "A 'C'? A 'B minus'? You can't possibly expect me to give you an 'A'?"

"I want to propose something that will make us both happy," Georgie said. "I want you to hire me back again. I want to be your apprentice."

Dominic Blackwell rode two more rounds in the Mirror Jumping that day on Cardinal and Polaris. Recovering from his earlier defeat, he won both with clear rounds and sparkling times on the clock. In the end, Polaris had the best time of the day. Second place went to Georgie on Belle with Dominic Blackwell taking third on Maximillion and a fourth on Cardinal.

The trophies and ribbons were handed out by the head of the Grand Prix USA organisation while Jilly Jones continued her commentary over the Tannoy.

"A remarkable story has unfolded here at the Kentucky Horse Park. The winning riders that you see here in the arena today are master and apprentice!

Young Georgie Parker just informed me that she is the protégée of Dominic Blackwell. She has been under his supervision at his stables and now we can see how his greatness has rubbed off on her! A memorable win for Team Blackwell – with all four places in the Mirror Jumping being awarded to members of their stables!"

In the arena, Georgie smiled at Dominic, who forced a smile in return, and then, in a gesture of crowd-pleasing solidarity, the two of them linked hands and raised their arms together in the air.

"You see?" Georgie muttered to Dominic under her breath. "I told you that I could make you look good if you played it my way."

"You're only my apprentice until the end of today," Blackwell muttered back. "Then I never want to see you again."

Georgie looked at him. "And what about my mark?"

Blackwell sighed. "You'll get your A," he said, struggling to maintain his fake mask of happiness, acutely aware that the crowds were looking at them. "I could hardly give less to my own apprentice, could I?"

Georgie smiled. "Thank you, Dominic. It's been a pleasure working with you."

"You blackmailed your way into an A!" Cameron Fraser just about fell off his seat in the Blainford dining room. It was Monday lunchtime before Tara's final class of the term. Georgie had just told the group about her Mirror Jumping showdown with her boss and the glowing report that he had given her.

Alex Chang looked at Georgie in stunned admiration. "You are unbelievable!" he said. "Beating Blackwell and getting an A for the privilege? That's gotta feel good!"

"I hate to be the one who points this out," Emily said, "but won't Kennedy tell on you?"

"I doubt it," Georgie said. "She got an A too because of Patricia. Plus, I let her grab the glory of being head girl for the term which will go on her school record. I think even Kennedy knows when to leave well enough alone."

"It's hardly fair though, is it?" Alex frowned. "I mean, we slogged our hearts out to get our marks!"

"Hey!" Georgie was genuinely hurt. "I earned that A in all kinds of hideous ways."

Georgie knew what Alex was driving at. These marks would inform Tara's end-of-term elimination.

"Actually," Cameron said. "I don't think any of you need to worry about elimination."

The others looked at him. Alice's face dropped. "Oh no, Cam! I thought everything was going really well with you and Frank Carsey?"

"It was – I mean, it is," Cameron said. "I've had the best time of my life in the past few weeks," he paused, "…and it's made me realise something. I've always loved cross-country, but I can't stand dressage. And to be a good eventing rider you have to be good at all phases these days. Besides, even on the cross-country course it was never the jumping for me – it was always just the speed, you know? Galloping as fast as you could go until the wind pins your horse's ears back and you're flying. And that's what it feels like when you're out there on the track."

He looked at his friends. "Frank says I've got what it takes – as long as I don't grow too much in the next three years, he's got a job for me when I leave Blainford."

"So you're dropping out of eventing class?" Alice frowned.

"Uh-huh," Cam nodded. "I've already told Tara. I'm swapping my major next year to racing."

"Me too," Daisy said. The others all turned to look at her.

"Well, not racing," Daisy clarified. "I'm swapping to polo. I told Tara last night."

"I didn't realise you were serious about polo," Emily said. "I mean, we all played last term and it's not like you were gagging to get back together for a game or anything."

"I'm not that into the low-goal stuff," Daisy shrugged. "But when I got to see the high-goal players, the way they play is totally different. It's amazing. When Seb rides, it's like the most exciting sport I've ever witnessed."

"So this is all about Seb!" Alice said. "I knew it!"

Daisy gave her a dark look. "Look, Alice, I don't want to date Seb – I want to *be* Seb. I want to be a proper player like him – at least three goals. I want to play for one of the big teams in Argentina and then maybe come home to England and set up my own team."

"Girls can't play at that high-goal level," Nicholas Laurent chipped in. Suddenly an entire table of girls were glaring at him.

"Nina Clarkin is a four-goal player," Daisy pointed out.

"Watch what you say, Laurent," Alice warned him, "unless you want the other leg broken."

Nicholas, who had only just had his cast taken off the week before, shifted uncomfortably in his seat.

"So is that it?" Alice looked around the table. "Anyone else leaving the ranks?"

Emily raised a hand. Everyone stared at her wide-eyed.

"Oh no!" Emily said hastily, "I didn't mean that I'm leaving. I just wanted to say that I heard Arden is. At least that's what Mindy Kershaw in Adelaide House told me. She said that Arden was signing up for Mrs Winton's class next year. She's going to major in grooming!"

And so, the final lesson of the term with Tara Kelly was not the brutal elimination the riders had been expecting. In the end, everyone had passed their apprenticeships – in one way or another. But the class of ten had still dwindled regardless. Only seven of them would continue through to the second year when the school returned in the late summer.

That last day in class Belle was a dream ride, balanced perfectly between her rider's hand and leg. Georgie thought back to the first term here at Blainford when the mare had been almost out of control when they attacked their fences. Now, they rode the course as a living breathing partnership.

"You and Belle looked very nice out there today," Tara told her as they were walking back to the stables. And then she added, "Almost as nice as you looked in the ring at the Kentucky Horse Park when you thrashed the pants off Dominic Blackwell."

"You were there?" Georgie was stunned.

"I saw you beat him," Tara said. "Even if Blackwell hadn't given you an A for your apprenticeship I would have given you a pass mark based on that last jump.

That turn with the flying change was nothing short of spectacular!"

By the end of the week exam marks had been handed out, final assessments had been made, exercise books and saddles had been packed away and the school was preparing for the summer holidays. To Georgie's relief, Kennedy had already left for her holiday in the Bahamas and Conrad was nowhere to be seen. On Friday morning Georgie went down to the stables with Emily and they watched as the farrier took the shoes off Barclay and Belle. Their horses would go barefoot in their fields for the next six weeks, turned out for a well-earned break until the new school year began.

For Georgie, who would spend the next six weeks at home in Gloucestershire, and Emily who was making the long journey home to New Zealand for the holidays, this summer holiday held a hidden sorrow. Belle and Barclay were both school horses – and there were no guarantees that students would get the same horses at Blainford for a second year.

Alice, who had already put Caspian on the horse truck ready to take him home to Maryland, accompanied Georgie as she led Belle down to her paddock for the last time.

Alice opened the gate and Georgie led Belle into the field. She stood there with her horse, reluctant to loosen the halter and let her go, fighting back the tears.

"It's a stupid, stupid rule," Georgie said bitterly as she stroked Belle's muzzle. "You come all the way across the world, they get you to bond with a horse, and then once you completely and utterly love it to bits they tell you next year you'll be with a new one!"

"Totally," Alice said comfortingly, "It's a dumb Blainford rule."

Alice had already put Caspian on the horse truck to take him home to Maryland. She was being supportive as she accompanied Georgie and Belle down to her paddock for the last time but the truth was that both the girls understood the logic behind Blainford's policy.

The school prided itself on turning out the world's

best professional riders. And pro-riders needed to learn to handle a wide variety of mounts. It wasn't enough to click with just one horse, and that was the reason for the Academy's rotation of school horses.

Georgie could see the sense in it, but that didn't make it any easier to accept. Faced with being separated from Belle for good, she found it impossible. As she stood there with the mare, she felt like her heart was breaking. She couldn't bring herself to remove the halter and let Belle go.

"I'm going to ask for you back," Georgie whispered to Belle. "I don't care about the rules. I'm going to ask Tara if I can have you again next year. I don't want another horse. I want you. "

Belle stood there gazing at her with those deep brown eyes and Georgie felt herself choking up with tears.

"OK," Alice said gently, "On the count of three, Georgie?"

She took hold of the strap of Belle's halter and slipped the buckle. "One… two… three!"

For a brief moment after Georgie slipped off the halter, Belle remained standing there. And then the realisation that she was free finally sunk in and the mare spun around on her hocks and took off.

It was a glorious summer day and Belle flung herself into a gallop along the length of the fenceline. She reached the end of the field and then she skidded to a halt, going straight up on her hind legs, flinging out her front feet, like a kitten playing with invisible string. In a sudden burst of speed, she came back again, making a wide loop around the two girls, letting loose a string of bucks, hooves high in the air.

"Whoah!" Alice's expression was awe-struck.

Georgie shook her head at Belle's raw power. "I'm so glad she doesn't act like that when I'm on her!"

The display of high-spirits had shaken away the gloom from the girls and there were no more tears as they put the halter away in the tack room and walked back down the driveway, leaving behind the red Georgian brick buildings of the main school as they headed to their boarding house.

Alice was gabbling on about her holiday plans, but then abruptly stopped. She had just seen the red pick-up truck parked outside Badminton House.

As Riley climbed out of the front seat of the pick-up, Alice gave him a wave and then bounded up the front steps.

"Hey, Riley! Can't talk – gotta go pack!"

"Hey, Alice, have a good holiday," Riley called after her, then he turned and saw Georgie looking pale, but pleased to see him.

Riley smiled. "I came to take you for a drive."

Georgie looked anxiously at her watch. Her flight home was leaving soon.

Riley opened the passenger door. "It won't take long," he said. "I want to show you something."

As they drove out of the gates of the Academy that afternoon the sun was warm and the air was still. The bluegrass fields were the prettiest Georgie had ever seen them as they drove down the back roads off the main route from Versailles and headed towards Pleasant Hill. Past the white post and rails, the red barns and the lush rolling pasture until they reached the crumpled pale green mailbox of Clemency Farm.

Riley pulled the pick-up to a stop at the gates.

"Look," he said to her.

A pair of tall stone gate posts had been erected at the entrance of the farm and a handsome wooden sign had been hung off the left-hand post. The sign was made from wood, painted white with gold trim and green writing that read: *Clemency Farm, home of Saratoga Firefly*.

And beneath that, in smaller type: *Property of John and Riley Conway*.

Georgie looked at the sign and smiled. "That's so great, Riley, having your name up there with your dad."

Riley frowned. "I didn't mean the sign, Georgie. Look over there."

He gestured past the gates to the front paddock of Clemency Farm. There, grazing in the field, was a brown yearling. Riley stuck his head out of the car window and made a clucking noise with his tongue and the horse raised its head. It was the prettiest young thing Georgie had ever seen.

"He's yours?"

Riley shook his head. "He is a 'she'. A filly. And she's not mine – she's ours."

He reached over and opened the glovebox and took out a piece of paper.

"I bought her under both of our names with some of the prize money from the Firecracker."

Georgie's eyes went wide as she looked at the registry form that Riley had handed her. "She's sired by Gifted and her dam is Paris Match," Riley continued. "Her racing name is right there on the papers."

Georgie's eyes scanned the form and found the filly's name. *Le Prix.*

"It's French," Riley said. "It means 'The Prize'. I figured that since her dad was called Gifted and she's kind of my gift to you for helping me win the Firecracker, it just sort of fits, you know?"

"Le Prix," Georgie said the name. "It's perfect for her."

The brown filly had been standing still, sniffing the air for a moment, and now she whinnied out to the horses over the far fence and broke into a trot towards them, her effortless strides covering the ground.

"She's beautiful, isn't she?" Riley said. "I haven't done anything with her yet. I thought I'd wait until you got back from England and then we could start training her together."

"She's amazing," Georgie said. "Thank you so much, Riley."

Staring at Le Prix, their future racing star, Georgie suddenly felt excited about flying back to England tomorrow. She couldn't wait to see her dad and Lucinda and Lily. She wanted to tell them everything that had happened. About the apprenticeship, and the Mirror Jumping and Riley winning the Firecracker. To tell them that she, Georgie Parker, now owned a genuine Kentucky bluegrass country filly with her name on the racing papers.

Riley put his arm around her. "What are you thinking?" he asked.

Georgie smiled. "They're never going to believe this back in Little Brampton."